THE SEARCH

WELL HOUSE
BOOKS

THE SEARCH

AN INSIDER'S NOVEL ABOUT A UNIVERSITY PRESIDENT

THOMAS EHRLICH

INDIANA UNIVERSITY PRESS

This book is a publication of

Indiana University Press
Office of Scholarly Publishing
Herman B Wells Library 350
1320 East 10th Street
Bloomington, Indiana 47405 USA

iupress.org

The paper used in this publication meets the minimum requirements of the American National Standard for Information Sciences—Permanence of Paper for Printed Library Materials, ANSI Z39.48-1992.

Manufactured in the United States of America

First printing 2024

Cataloging information is available from the Library of Congress.

hdbk: 978-0-253-07031-9
pbk: 978-0-253-07032-6
web pdf: 978-0-253-07033-3

To Indiana University—thanks for the memories

CONTENTS

PREFACE

I had the great pleasure and privilege of being president of Indiana University (IU). My wife, Ellen, and I loved our time at IU. Not every minute of every day, of course. No job offers that, even this one, which I viewed as a calling. But for us, our time in Indiana was a joy.

We arrived at IU in the summer of 1987. Earlier that spring, the IU men's basketball team won the NCAA basketball championship under Coach Bob Knight. Later that year, under Coach Bill Mallory, our football team went to the first of four bowl games while I was president. I love intercollegiate sports and knew I would have a full plate at IU. Sports provide life lessons and pleasure for the players as well as a festival spirit for a campus and enjoyment for the fans. Ellen and I worked closely at IU with colleagues who became our dear friends. We are still in touch with many of them, though we left IU in 1994.

Ellen was born and grew up in and near Chicago. But I lived in New England all my life until we were married. At IU, I learned hallmarks of the Midwest: a deep sense of caring and kindness for all those in our community, a strong work ethic, and a lack of pretentions and cant. There's a saying that no one is more passionately committed than a convert, whether to a place or cause. Although neither Ellen nor I grew up in Indiana, we became committed Hoosiers.

For the first time, Ellen and I were able to work closely together. That pleasure is reflected in this novel. We traveled as a team to every part of Indiana and beyond on behalf of IU. We hosted hundreds of events at every one of IU's eight campuses. Distinguished national and international guests, like Yo-Yo Ma and the president of Costa Rica, stayed at Bryan House, our lovely home on the IU campus in Bloomington. We entertained scores of Indiana legislators and others at Lilly House, the stately house that Eli Lilly left to the university in Indianapolis, and where we stayed when the legislature was in session.

We learned how much citizens of Indiana cared about Indiana University. Whether or not they attended IU, it was "theirs." When I made mistakes, as I certainly did, they picked me up and put me back on my feet and on the right track.

Ellen and I each had our separate roles to support the university as well as our joint roles. Ellen became head of United Way in Monroe Country, where IU–Bloomington is located. She later joined the United Way board there, then the Indiana State board, and finally the national United Way board.

I was able realize a dream I had of leading a great public university. I graduated from Harvard College and Harvard Law School; I had been dean of Stanford Law School and provost of the University of Pennsylvania. But I believed deeply in public education and wanted the chance to lead a public university, with all its challenges and opportunities. IU gave me that chance, and I am forever grateful. And I was proud of what I was able to accomplish in collaboration with IU's faculty, staff, trustees, alumni, and other friends.

After seven wonderful years at IU, we decided to return to California. We missed our three children and wanted to be close to them and to our nine grandchildren as they grew up. Ellen and one of our sons had open-heart surgery at the IU hospital in Indianapolis. These events, both of which turned out well, helped make going back to our family a priority. And at age sixty, I wanted an opportunity to return to full-time teaching and writing. While I was able to do some of both at IU, my primary focus, of course, was my role as president.

So why did I write a novel about a president of a public midwestern university rather than reflections on my years at Indiana University? Three reasons were primary, apart from the fact that I had already written a short book about key issues during my time at IU (*The Courage to Inquire,* Indiana University Press, 1995).

First, I had authored nonfiction books, particularly about education, but I had never written a novel before. When COVID-19 struck, I no longer had access to the research materials I would need for another nonfiction book. So I thought it would be fun to try to write a novel. My last foray into fiction had been in high school. I took a creative writing course via Zoom at Stanford University, which is near when Ellen and I now live and where I still teach. Writing a novel could test my abilities to learn a whole new set of writing skills.

Ellen and I have read hundreds of novels in our sixty-six years of marriage. Our favorites are nineteenth-century greats—George Eliot, Thomas Hardy, and Anthony Trollope. Although I knew I could never come close to matching their prose, I thought the challenge of fiction would be a great learning experience. It was that and more. It was a delight. And in the process of writing, I gained both insights and respect for master novelists. Second, over my years at IU, I often struggled when friends asked me what it was like to be president of a big public university. They would often add, for emphasis, "What's it *really* like?" In response, I'd use words like "challenging" and then tell a story or two. Stories, I think, are the most powerful form of teaching, though narrative is rarely honored in the academy.

But I could never in a story or two capture what being a public university president really *felt* like. How exhilarating it was when I could see that decisions I had made at IU made a real difference in the lives of students, faculty, and staff. It's like the pop of a flash bulb when I am teaching a class and a student suddenly gains mastery of a complex concept. Light bulbs were going off all the time and all around me as president. I felt I was a kind of institutional architect or orchestra conductor, helping students and faculty strengthen their ideas and put them into practice. But a simple chronicle of important happenings at a university and the president's role in facilitating some of those happenings rarely sound exciting when read on paper.

Time and again at IU, I found that faculty members would identify a problem and suggest ways to fix that problem. These happenings would never be recorded in a history of a university or memoir of a president. And the faculty were rarely seeking credit for their help. They were just meeting their responsibilities, recognizing that those responsibilities involved strengthening the IU community. When that happened, the feelings that often washed over me were pride in the university and appreciation for my good fortune.

Not all my feelings as IU president were positive, of course, and some of my irritations are reflected in this novel, though the context, characters, and issues are changed. Most obvious, over my years at IU, many search committees reported their recommendations to me. Searches for chancellors of the IU campuses, for example, were often difficult because no one on the committees really knew the full range of what the chancellors did. Committee members often valued their interview with a candidate much more that the evidence of what others said who had worked with that person. In practice, I had to praise the committees for their hard work—and they did work hard—but find ways to probe the issues they simply ignored. I solved that irritating problem in the novel by including in the search for a new football coach/athletic director two athletic directors from other campuses. But a step like that rarely happens in reality.

As IU president, part of my job was being sure the trustees had something important to do, other than consider whether to fire me, as the trustees consider firing the president in my novel. There always were serious policy issues to discuss with IU trustees, who often were closer to political winds than I was. But sometimes I found myself furious when a trustee proposed handling an academic issue in ways I knew the faculty could not, and should not, accept. The problem was exacerbated by the small size of the IU board, like the others in the Big Ten and in my novel. One trustee's complaint can be an irritant. But if a second trustee echoes that complaint, it can be disaster for the president unless a compromise can be found. And that can be difficult in part because almost everything that happens at a public university is public, as it should be. When this happened, I often felt frustrated in the extreme.

I recognize the dangers in the former president of a big public university writing a novel about what it is like to be a president of a big public university. Readers may think that I wrote a chronicle about what happened when I was president of IU. I did not. Some of the stories I tell in the novel have elements that happened. Some of the characters have features that I encountered at IU. But the persons and events portrayed are fictional, though the discerning reader may note some correspondences to events and personages from my years there.

I do hope my novel gives readers a sense of what it felt like as a university president to grapple with the kinds of challenges and personalities I faced. Some of the issues that are center stage for Charlie Rosen, the president of fictional Nebraska State University in my novel, are ones I also faced. More of those issues are completely fictional. But all the issues triggered the kinds of emotions I felt at various times as IU president.

The third reason for writing this novel was to underscore my concern about the corrosive impact of money on Division I intercollegiate athletics. My concern began not long after I arrived at IU. I was told that the top priority for new university facilities was an indoor football-practice facility. When I naively asked the athletic director why the facility was needed, since football is always played outside, the answer was that IU's rivals had those facilities. And IU needed them to compete.

My concern deepened in 1990 when Penn State joined the Big Ten Conference. At the time, the proponents rightly argued that the addition of Penn State would substantially increase TV revenues for the conference. Harold Shapiro, then president of the University of Michigan, and I objected on the ground that travel between the two universities would take students away from their home campuses for too long.

The lure of increased revenues has rapidly escalated since then. The invitation to UCLA, USC, and the Universities of Oregon and Washington to join the Big Ten, and the much longer trips involved for athletes, is one example. Money for athletics has been increasingly undercutting the academic purposes of universities as their student athletes increasingly become paid gladiators and some of their coaches become multimillionaires. An accelerating arms race is underway to pay coaches more and more millions of dollars and to build more and more expensive athletic facilities, though athletic revenues exceed expenses at only a handful of campuses.

This novel is not narrowly about money and big-time athletics. But an overarching theme is the struggles of a public-university president to maintain the primacy of academics over athletics. The novel is also not about football. But I hope it reveals my own ambivalence about the sport. On the one hand, I love watching it. On the other hand, I am well aware of the physical risks it brings to players, risks that may leave them with mental and physical scars for the rest of their lives.

Finally, my hope is that this novel gives readers some of the same pleasure that writing it gave me.

Tom Ehrlich

THE SEARCH

Prologue

If you know anything about college football, you know about "Buddy" Knowland, the legendary coach of Nebraska State University. He was just enshrined in the College Football Hall of Fame in Atlanta, Georgia, almost ten years to the day after his last game. To be eligible, coaches must have a minimum of ten years of head coaching experience, have coached one hundred or more games, and have won a least 60 percent of those games. Knowland met those requirements easily.

You may also have heard that Knowland and I clashed when I was president of Nebraska State. That's an understatement, but it will do for now. I knew that the Hall of Fame ceremony would trigger an avalanche of articles about Knowland and his winning ways. And that is just what has happened.

In the wake of that publicity, the director of the Nebraska State University Press suggested I write my story about the challenges I faced as president of Nebraska State, particularly the challenge of choosing a successor to Knowland. This is that story.

It's easy for me to set one part of the record straight. My name is Charlie Rosen. Not Charles Rosen. I've never been sure why my mother insisted on "Charlie." She just told me she liked the name. But all my life I have had to correct people who, trying to be proper, misaddress me as "Mr. Charles Rosen." In the army, I had to write, "Charlie NMI Rosen," to make clear I have no middle initial.

To start my story, you should know about how and why Knowland and I clashed. I was well aware, long before I first came to Nebraska State as a student, that football is king on the campus. I knew it's not as big as football at our rival, the University of Nebraska, of course—nothing outside of Alabama is that big. But I certainly realized that our football teams did extremely well in its conference under Knowland's leadership. His teams never had a losing season, were the conference champions eleven times, and won a majority of bowl games in which they played.

Knowland was a big man, standing six feet four inches tall, with a face and nose that looked flattened by running into a wall at an early age. And he was a foul-mouthed bully who screamed expletives at his players on and off the field. "You're a shit-ass sissy," was his frequent line when he thought a player had not tackled hard enough. I once quipped, "The university teaches sixty-seven languages, but Knowland's is not one of them."

Knowland was also a misogynist and frequently made clear, in language strewn with obscenities, that he thought women were inferior beings. He was known for his advice to his players: "Big tits and little ass—that's the way I like them, and you should too."

My predecessor, Enzo Enrico, regularly watched and listened to Knowland in team practices and in the locker room after games, so I decided it would be wise for me to do the same thing. I was shocked the first time. Knowland had his own form of abuse that was always on the edge of being out of control, and sometimes over that edge. I admit that most students who survived Knowland's screaming played better than they could have thought possible. But many players dropped out after hearing Knowland's continual ranting.

Fear is a terrible way to motivate anyone to learn. I had more than enough of fear and being yelled at when I was drafted during the Vietnam War and was regularly verbally abused by my sergeant. I can still remember the sergeant screaming at me to go into a dense cluster of bushes when we were on maneuvers in Texas. I told him the bushes were full of poison ivy, and I was extremely allergic. But he replied that I would be peeling potatoes for a month if I did not go. I went into the bushes and spent ten days in the hospital covered with poison ivy.

I did battle with Knowland since the first day I became president. Really, even before that. I'm the first Jewish president of the university. Nebraska has fewer than ten thousand Jews in a population of almost two million. When I was chosen, I looked at the schedule of events for the year and realized that homecoming was scheduled on Yom Kippur. The main event would be the annual football game with our archrival, the University of Nebraska.

I quickly called the chair of the board, Franklin Adams. "I know it's important for me to be at the game, along with the festivities before and afterward. It is a perfect time for me to meet and greet alumni. But for me to be there, the date has to be changed, since Yom Kippur is the holiest day in the year for Jews." Adams did not have to be told more and assured me that homecoming would be switched to another home game. That happened, but not without a furious call from Knowland. "What in the world are you thinking?" he said. "The Athletic Department is not made of money. We hold our events on Easter and even on Christmas. What is so special about Yom Kippur? I can't begin to think how many events will have to be rescheduled and how expensive the shifts will be." So we got off on the wrong foot and stayed that way.

Knowland and I crossed verbal swords again, just after the first football game of my initial year as president. Nebraska State athletic teams were called "the Hogs" then. The nickname dated back to the establishment of Nebraska State University in the mid-nineteenth century. The Nebraska legislature created the university when Clarence Rossiter, the largest hog farmer in the country at the time, gave the land and funding for the initial set of university facilities. The nickname was the idea of the first president of Nebraska State as a tribute to Rossiter and his generosity.

I had noticed watching Nebraska State football games that the other teams we played, and particularly their fans during away games, ridiculed the label. "Oink, oink, oink," was the frequent chant I heard over and over again.

Just before that first game, the student newspaper, *The Sentinel*, published an editorial urging that the nickname was an embarrassment and should be changed. I thought the editorial was right on target. So

I called Knowland and said I wanted to have a competition to choose a new nickname. I said being called "the Hogs" was a humiliation that long ago should have been corrected.

Knowland exploded in response. "Don't you understand the tradition that 'the Hogs' represent. It's our badge of pride! It's the symbol of our heritage! Would you want to change the 'Boilermakers' of Purdue or the 'Ducks' of Oregon because those names embarrassed you? Every true Nebraska State fan says he's a hog with pride."

We went back and forth for a few minutes, each getting angrier and angrier, but it was clear that Knowland was not going to budge. Reluctantly, I decided to let the matter go, though I was irritated at myself for doing so.

Knowland and I clashed once more within months of my appointment as president. The issue seemed to me minor at the time, but not to Knowland. The university had a rule that the Athletic Department's compliance officer, Jenny Stern—the person in charge of ensuring that NCAA rules are followed—must report any issues of noncompliance to the president as well as the athletic director. Each player on the football team received four free tickets for each home game, and most players gave them to their girlfriends or families. But just after my inauguration, I received a report from Jenny that our star tailback, Terry Razoski, a runner-up all-American, had sold two of his tickets before a game, which violated the NCAA rule book. I immediately asked Polly Porter, my executive assistant, to schedule an appointment in my office to meet with Knowland. I felt I had no choice: a NCAA rule was violated, and the university was obligated to report it.

For the eleven years Enrico was president, he never criticized anything Knowland did, but rather showered him with public praise. Knowland was paid $1.5 million as football coach and another $600,000 as athletic director, far more than my compensation and more than the salaries of either the dean of our medical school or the head of our hospital. Knowland also received a car, a generous expense account, and another million dollars from a radio show and his endorsement of various items of football gear. Those items all had the Nebraska State logo on them, as well as Adidas's, which sponsors our teams. But that did not stop Knowland from holding them up and saying in front of a TV camera that he personally chose them for his championship team.

I had not known that Enrico always went to Knowland's office when they were scheduled to meet, the implication being that Knowland was more important than Enrico. If I had realized that, I might have continued the practice, since I knew Knowland had an explosive temper and that he would already be furious that the player's misdeed could hurt the football team's chances in the fall. So when Knowland walked into my office, he was fuming.

This was our first meeting, and I tried some small talk to start. But he would have none of that. "I hope you are not going to tell the NCAA about this," he told me even before he sat down.

"But the rules require the university to do so," I responded. "We do not have a choice." Without meaning to, I know I raised my voice sharply.

Knowland countered by saying that, at that point, we were the only ones who knew about the sale, along with the Razoski, a football trainer, and the compliance officer. The trainer had learned about the sale from Razoski, and the trainer told the compliance officer.

I remembered Knowland's exact words in response. "The requirements are so goddamned complicated that no one can keep track of them," he said. "It's a stupid rule, and I doubt Razoski knew the rule."

At that point I lost my temper. Stern had told me that every member of the football and basketball teams had heard directly from her that selling their tickets was a violation of the rules. I blew up in anger and said, "You know that's not true!" He got even madder and told me that if we reported the violation to the NCAA, Razoski would be forced to miss the last two games of the season, including the Apple Bowl. "All right," I told Knowland. "But never let this happen again."

I knew I was making a moral mistake the moment I said that. And I promised myself never to do that again. And I never did.

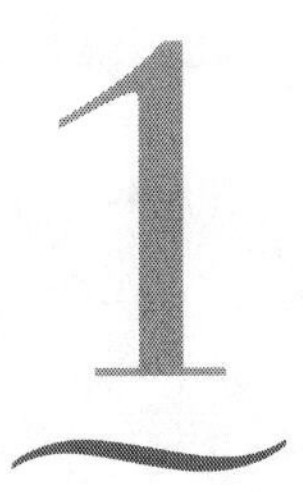

The stadium announcer spoke in measured tones. "It is my sad duty," he said, as over eighty thousand football fans fell silent, "to announce that our beloved Coach Knowland has died. He was the finest coach in the history of Nebraska State University football, and he's gone to his great reward. All of us know it will be a great one. Please stand for a moment of silent prayer." The crowd let out a collective sound of anguish. Then the stadium fell silent, though I could hear small groups of fans talking softly around me. Some had started to sob.

Cringing, I jumped up from my seat in the President's Sky Box, which is slung like a blue zeppelin above the top rows of stadium seats, and nodded to the donors sitting with me for this last game of the season, the all-important one against the University of Nebraska, known as the U of N.

"I've got to go," I said to my wife, Emma. "Can you take care of things here? I don't even know if they'll finish the game."

"I'll do my best," she said as she squeezed my hand.

When the announcer spoke, our Nebraska State team was ahead 34–32, with seconds left before the end of the third quarter. The U of N kicker had just attempted a field goal from our 20-yard line. One of our defensive linemen leaped and blocked the kick. But a referee blew his whistle and signaled the lineman had been offside. Knowland had raced onto the field, snarling with anger at the call, and our fans screamed with him. The noise was deafening. Suddenly, Knowland crumpled to the ground. He tried to raise himself. Then he collapsed and lay still.

Our team doctor, who was always on the sidelines during games, rushed onto the field. He's a big man, a former star halfback on one of Knowland's first teams. A cluster of assistant coaches followed. Then scores of players surrounded the prostrate Knowland, the coaches, and the other players. Those of us in the stadium could not see what was happening. Only about ten minutes passed until the announcer intoned, "It is my sad duty," but it seemed like an hour.

Later I learned that the doctor tried CPR for several minutes. Knowland opened his eyes for a few seconds and whispered, "Keep playing." And then he died. He had suffered a massive heart attack.

I raced down three flights of stairs in the stadium to the ground floor and rushed onto the playing field because that was the quickest way to reach our team's locker room on the other side of the field. I knew the elevator would take too long. As I came onto the field, I heard angry yelling. "You killed Coach!" and "You've got blood on your hands!"

I ran across the field and into the graffiti-scarred tunnel that leads off the field to our team's locker room. Bright blue banners on all the walls marked the success of Knowland's teams. Talking stopped as I walked in. I was afraid some players or even coaches might try to keep me out. But no one did. Rather, they all looked down at the floor as I spoke. "Players, coaches, trainers, I know you loved Coach Knowland as well as respected him. I know he made each player play better than he thought he could, and his coaching made each coach a better coach than he thought possible. Coach Knowland and I had our differences. I'm sure you know that. But those differences fade in the face of this great tragedy. My heart is with you all in this hour of grief." Then I left the locker room. As I made my way out, one of the trainers told me about Knowland's last words. "I am sure the team will respect Coach's wishes," he said.

Sure enough, by the time I got back to the President's Sky Box, the announcer had told the crowd that the game would go on. "That was

Coach Knowland's dying wish. The players and coaches on both sides all want to respect that."

The game did resume for the final quarter, and our team played with a ferociousness that struck everyone in the stadium. We were penalized eight times, and two University of Nebraska players were carried off the field unconscious. But we won 48–32. This was our first victory over the University of Nebraska in eleven years.

At the final whistle, Emma and I walked slowly down the stairs and out of the stadium. As we headed toward the president's house in the middle of campus, I mused with Emma about what would happen next. "You know what a real son of a bitch, he was," I said, "but his fans were so fooled by him and blinded by his wins. Here and around Nebraska, they all loved him. But because of our battles, I'm going to get blamed for his heart attack, and so for his death. I'm so pissed off. I can just smell it. Rumors must be brewing already. They are going to push me out for this. For so many times I held my temper during his antics when I could and should have wacked him. Now I'll never have the chance. Even if I survive as president, will Knowland's ghost haunt me forever?"

Emma grabbed my arm, pulled me to a stop, and gave me a big kiss on the lips. I was stunned for a minute. We never show our love for each other that openly in public. "Stop imagining the worst," she said. "And whatever happens, we're in this together—Charlie and Emma Rosen."

Emma was the only person at Nebraska State with whom I could be totally frank about what was going through my head. "The next days, maybe weeks or even months, are going to be tough," she said. "If you lose the presidency, that's not the worst thing that could happen to us. You would be leaving with your integrity intact. That's more than some college presidents can say. In round one of your fights with Knowland, you let him push you around; your ethics were the loser, and you were up all night worrying about it. I know you won't let that happen again. That said, I would really miss the chances we have at Nebraska State to do so many things together as real partners. And I would miss this house as well."

Around midnight, I heard chanting outside the president's house, and almost at the same time, my private telephone line rang. Calls to my publicly listed line went directly to my administrative assistant, Polly Porter, and the callers were told I was busy at the moment, and I or my office would be back in touch as soon as possible. Occasionally, Polly asked if I wanted to respond, but generally, she did in my name and then told me what she had said. She had perfect judgment in this arena.

The call was from the campus police chief. "A large band of students are marching toward your home and will be there momentarily," she said. "We have our officers stationed around your house, and I don't think there is any danger except to your sleep." Sure enough, in another minute we heard voices chanting, "Rosen, Rosen, time to go, go, go," and "Rosen, Rosen, you'll be frozen."

The students did no damage except for trampling flowers in our beautiful garden, but Emma and I were shaken. My blood was boiling when I realized our twin girls, Abby and Amy, were in tears. Our aged golden retriever, Becky, who would usually love to be petted by students as they walked by our house going to and from classes, was barking in terror.

The next morning, Sunday, the clouds over my head got darker. Knowland had become a statewide hero. "He died with his cleats on" was the banner headline in our local paper. And the paper reported that a drive had already been started to raise money for a full-sized statue to be made of Knowland holding a football in his hand, to be placed in front of the football stadium. The paper added that there was also a growing chorus of demands that the football stadium be named for Knowland. And there were a dozen letters to the editor calling for the trustees to fire me.

At 8:00 a.m., the vice president for facilities, Sally Eshkanazi, called to say that Sonny Tizzo—Knowland's associate athletic director, assistant football coach, and general factotum—was on the line. She transferred the call to me. "The Knowland family has delegated me to ask for approval to use of the football stadium for Coach's funeral service tomorrow morning. They want the funeral right away, so fans who came from across the country to watch the game yesterday can stay and attend the funeral to pay their last respects. The stadium is the fitting place for the service. It is also the only place with enough room to hold those who will want to attend." I felt I had little choice but to approve.

Later that morning, around nine o'clock, the chair of the trustees, Franklin Adams, telephoned to tell me the board wanted to hold an emergency meeting the next afternoon, right after the Knowland funeral, to discuss "your situation." I knew that "your situation" were code words for whether the board would fire me. "You know I'll do everything I can to keep you, Charlie," he said. "But you and your fiery clashes with Knowland haven't made it easy for me."

Adams insisted the trustees meet in my office, in the Administration Building, rather than at Trustee House, where they usually met, on the ground, he told the other trustees, that reporters would be hanging around Trustee House to see what might happen there. But Adams later confided to me his real reason was he thought it would be tougher to fire me at a meeting in my own office.

Adams was executive vice president of the largest company in Nebraska, Adams Tractors, one of only five Fortune 500 companies in the state. He had been chosen as a trustee by governors, Republican and Democratic, and then selected as chair by the other trustees, for the past twenty-four years. He had, by the sheer force of his intellect and personality, successfully kept the university immune from partisan political squabbles. His wavy white hair was always elegantly groomed, and he wore only three-piece suits that stood out as much as my bow ties. And he was deeply respected by everyone, including all the board members. That was the one thing I knew I had going for me.

The funeral on Monday morning, starting at 10:00 a.m., was the largest happening in Nebraska state history apart from athletic events. It was a clear, crisp fall day, and over sixty-five thousand mourners filled the stadium seats, with thousands more standing on the field. The Episcopal bishop for our area presided. Overnight, a giant platform had been raised in the middle of the stadium field. On the platform, together with the Knowland family—his wife and seven sons—was the entire football team, coaching and support staff, trustees, and university officers. Nine speakers talked for over two hours—the bishop, the Nebraska lieutenant governor (a personal friend of Knowland), three of Knowland's sons, Sonny Tizzo, and three players from three of Knowland's conference championship teams. Needless to say, I was not asked to speak.

Many students and fans had brought large banners. "Good-bye, Coach. We'll see you upstairs," said one. Others read: "Wrong-way Rosen can't bother you now." "You're the best thing that ever happened at Nebraska State." And more, much more. Finally, it was over, but not before all three sons who spoke implied they thought I had at least contributed to Knowland's death and perhaps actually killed him by interfering with his management of Nebraska State athletics. "Dad always stood up for what was right," one said, "and he knew that it was right that Nebraska State athletics should be handled by the athletic director, without interference by the university president." Another son was harsher. "My father was so often shackled when he was trying to do his best for Nebraska State and all its teams. Why don't university administrators ever learn to let big-time athletics stay in the hands of those who know something about them."

Do they have a point? I thought to myself. Knowland coached his players to be better than they thought possible. He gave great entertainment to our students and fans in Nebraska and beyond. He strengthened ties between Nebraska State and its alumni. And he was a bastard. So what? Why should I have cared so much about that? I had the whole university to run. Why couldn't I leave athletics alone? Why couldn't I be just like most other dogs in the intercollegiate kennel and let that bone alone?

Was it, at least in part, because I was small? I was barely five feet seven inches tall with shoes on and weighed only 130 pounds. And I'd had polio as a boy, which made my right leg a full inch shorter than the left. I wore a lift in my right shoe but still walked with a mild limp. Growing up on a soybean farm on the Nebraska plains, I had a hard time doing any sports and was regularly called "gimp" by my classmates. The fact that I was also a good student made boys in my class eager to make fun of me whenever they could.

Or was it because I had a quick temper, which I lost the first time I met with Knowland? He looked stunned when I did because he was used to my predecessor, whose only role in intercollegiate athletics was as cheerleader. I had struggled to control that temper all my life. How did I get that temper? Was it nature or nurture? Both, I think. My father exploded with his fists at my mother, my sister, or me whenever he had too much to drink, which was often. I frequently saw my mother with bruises on her arms and face. She always had an excuse—such as she tripped. But I was sure my father hit her. That's one reason since my undergraduate days I have never drunk alcohol. At parties and receptions, I ask for nonalcoholic wine or beer, and no one knows the difference.

As a boy, I learned to act tough, because otherwise other boys would taunt me and push me around. I even took boxing lessons one summer to learn how to protect myself. My temper frequently led to fights with schoolmates, and I have a broken nose that never correctly healed to prove it.

It was when I was a sophomore at Nebraska State that my temper really got me into trouble. It was at about two or three in the morning at my fraternity house, Tau Delta Phi, which is a Jewish fraternity, started when Jews were precluded from membership in other fraternities. Fraternity brothers are supposed to support each other, but from the first time we met, Leonard Lyons and I disliked each other, though I'm not sure why. Perhaps because I was a lot smarter than he was, and he was a star basketball player, while I was never even moderately good at any sport except tennis doubles. My limp didn't impede me in that sport.

Lyons was drunk when he came into our fraternity common room, where I was reading. He began heckling me because I didn't drink. "You may be dry, but you're a wet blanket," he kept repeating. I got so mad that I grabbed the bottle of gin out of his hand and drank straight from the bottle. In a few minutes, I was drunk as well.

Then we got in a silly argument about whether college athletes were more successful in business than other people. He started taunting me, saying over and over again, "Your leg is limp, and I bet your pecker is too." After the third or fourth time, I got so mad I picked up my fraternity paddle and wacked him on his arm, breaking it in three places. He fell down screaming. No one else was around, and I half carried, half dragged him to my car and drove him to the hospital. He needed a series of operations and could not play basketball again.

University officials never learned of this incident, but it quickly became known to everyone in the fraternity. I was brought before the fraternity officers for a hearing. My best friend at the fraternity was Jay Jacobs—a friend from our high school days. He was a tall, handsome guy, with long blond hair that he kept in a ponytail, to the great amusement of the rest of our fraternity brothers. Jacobs was my unofficial defense attorney at the hearing, and he made the case that Lyons was equally at fault since he had cruelly taunted me while we were both drunk. After some debate, the fraternity officers decided it would be best to do nothing and hope that word of what happened would not spread across the campus. Fortunately, it didn't.

My parents paid for Lyons's medical expenses on the understanding he would keep quiet about our fight. Periodically after that he would ask me for a "loan" of a few thousand dollars, saying he would tell the full story to the newspaper if I refused. I always paid. After a while, I stopped hearing from Lyons. As the years passed, and I was in increasingly senior positions in my career, I worried from time to time that Lyons would publicize my misdeed. But after I did not hear from him for many years, I almost forgot the incident. And I did not drink alcohol again.

I never told Emma of my run-in with Lyons. Mostly, I think, I was just ashamed of what I had done and didn't want to embarrass myself by confessing what a jerk I had been. But I also was avoiding reminding Emma of my temper.

My temper tantrums, as Emma calls them, have been held in check most of the time since we were married. Emma would not go through with our planned wedding unless I swore I would keep my temper under wraps. She kept reminding me of those great lines by Reinhold Niebuhr: "God grant me the serenity to accept the things I cannot change, the courage to change the things I can, and the wisdom to know the difference."

My promise was made after the hotel where the wedding was taking place canceled our booking, claiming a mistake. I was so furious I screamed in rage at the hotel manager and threw the front-desk call bell across the hotel lobby. Emma was mortified. She was much more upset at me than at the hotel. And with my marriage on the line, I assured her it would not happen again. It rarely did. When I did lose my temper, I apologized and tried to make up with the object of my anger before Emma heard about it. But Knowland was a trigger for my temper I could not control. Something inside me could not let this loud-mouthed bully push me around.

2

As I sat waiting in my office for the trustees' emergency meeting to begin, with my future as president in the balance, I mused about how and why Knowland and I came to clash so often, for I knew the trustees would demand a full accounting. Fortunately, I keep a diary, and it included a blow-by-blow account of our clashes.

Ironically, I indirectly owed my job as president to Knowland, much as I came to loath him. My predecessor, Enzo Enrico, had been president for sixteen years, and had never criticized Knowland, though Knowland had given him plenty of cause for doing so. But a year before my appointment, the former athletic director had retired, and Knowland demanded that he be appointed to that position while he retained his role as football coach. If he didn't get the job, he said he would quit Nebraska State and go elsewhere. Since he was regularly being recruited by other major universities, this was no ideal threat. But Enrico refused, saying Knowland had to choose which job he wanted, but he couldn't have both. I always thought that was a gutsy thing for Enrico to do, especially since he was a mild-mannered guy who had never clashed with Knowland before.

But Knowland went straight to the Board of Trustees and told them he would be gone unless he could have both jobs. The trustees overruled Enrico, who promptly resigned effective upon the appointment of the successor. And for reasons I'll explain later, the Trustees chose me to succeed him. Should I have realized that I, too, would soon have deep trouble with Knowland, just as Enrico did? In retrospect, I should have. But I naively thought I could handle him.

I wanted a better record of this meeting with the trustees in my office than my memory might provide. So I secretly recorded it. Was that wise or fair to the trustees? Maybe not, but if I was going to get fired, I wanted a record of exactly what was said by whom. I had a five-year contract as president, and I was only halfway through my third year. My contract said I could be fired at any time, but unless there was "dereliction of duties as president," I would be paid for the full term of my contract. Even if the trustees decided to remove me, I knew it could not be for "dereliction of duties."

My office was cavernous and decorated the way a longtime president in the 1960s and 1970s had wanted. Not much had changed since then, though I kept hoping a wealthy donor would visit me, say the office needed a redo, and offer to pay for it. The office had a huge table at one end that sat ten people, and my desk was at the other. A short wall next to my desk was filled with pictures of my family, and other family photos were on the desk.

The desk is an elaborately carved English partners' piece, brought across the ocean and then to Nebraska by the university's first president. I wished I could have exchanged it for the modern desk I'd seen by the contemporary craftsman Thomas Moser. That desk was elegant in its simplicity: a plain slab of polished walnut, held up by thin, curving legs, which supported two drawers on each side in a way that made it seem the drawers were floating. Woodworking was one of my hobbies, but I never made anything with anywhere near the grace of that desk.

In the middle of the office was a circle of two sofas flanked on each side by two wooden chairs. It had been redecorated by Sally Enrico, the wife of my predecessor. Except for removing heavy dark drapes, changing the art on the walls, and adding some bookcases—Enrico did not read much—I hadn't wanted to spend the university's money to redecorate. A university president I know was canned for spending too much on redecoration, and I did not want to take that risk. But the office was too imperious for me; it reflected Enrico's personality. And I wished the walls were off-white, not a pale yellow that looked too much like urine.

A small, book-lined study with no telephone or computer was attached to my office. I went there most mornings from 8:00 a.m. to 10:00 a.m. to think and plan with nothing more than a pen and pad of paper. I told my colleagues that this time was sacred for me—away from distractions—so I could reflect on the handful of key challenges facing the university and not get caught up in meetings, emails, and day-to-day issues that would otherwise consume my time. But I suspected that some of my staff thought I just liked to sleep late. And sometimes I did.

Emma was a wonderful artist, and six of her stunning paintings were on the office walls. I knew many, maybe most, who visited me in the office did not like her big, abstract pictures and would much have preferred the Nebraska impressionist artists that had been hung when Enrico was president. But the art in my office was one of the few matters I could comfortably decide without consulting anyone.

Like most large, public universities in the Midwest, Nebraska State University had a small board of trustees. Three were elected by the alumni, three were appointed by the governor, and one was a student appointed by the president. The student served for one year while the rest served for three years, and their terms were staggered.

The chair of the board, Franklin Adams, had been first nominated by a Republican governor in 1994. He was executive vice president of the largest manufacturer of agricultural machinery in Nebraska, but he spent over half his time on university affairs, and I viewed him as an ally when I was chosen as president. Fortunately for me, Adams was on good terms with Knowland. He admired Knowland's talents, while recognizing the coach's limitations.

I knew my tenure as president was on the line. I thought I could count on three votes to support me: Adams; Patricia Sencor, who was also appointed by the governor; and Henry Washington, the student trustee. Sencor had told me at one of my first trustee meetings that she was, in her words, "appalled by the numbers of injuries on the football field, especially concussions that likely cause permanent brain damage." Washington had impressed me since he transferred from a local community college in his junior year. He was Black and came from the South Side of Chicago. When we first talked, he made clear he thought Black players on the football and basketball teams were exploited by their coaches, so I knew he was no fan of Knowland.

I also knew that the three trustees elected by the alumni were likely to oppose me—Jared Carter, Preston Anchor, and Samuel Tyson. All three were former football players for Knowland, and they had been elected because their names were known throughout Nebraska as having been star players on championship teams.

This meant that my fate was probably in the hands of the one remaining gubernatorial appointee, Felicity Sergeant. She was a handsome, blond woman in her mid-fifties. She was cochair of the governor's reelection campaign two years earlier. I knew she was very close to the governor and might well have consulted with him about my fate. Twenty years earlier, she started the most successful advertising firm in Nebraska. Over the past two years, she had been pressing me hard to make better use of social media to promote Nebraska State. I knew she was right but had found it tough to find PR persons who knew something about both higher education and social media. Sergeant liked to wear black pants and gaudy print tops, often in various shades of blue, the Nebraska State color. She had a sharp tongue and took quick offense when she thought her views were not being taken sufficiently seriously among the other trustees—as often happened.

I could tell when I sat down at the large conference table in my office that Carter, Anchor, and Tyson had planned together how to remove me because they kept whispering to each other. Anchor was the oldest of the three and was the natural leader among them. He was a tall, lanky man, one who had not gone soft after his decades away from being a starting tight end on a Knowland team. Since then he had run the large cement company that his father started and that made him a rich man. He was dressed in a dark blue suit and a white shirt. That was the uniform of the day for the Knowland funeral, which had been that morning. When I wore a tie, it was always a bow tie, and when

Anchor was elected as a trustee the year before, the first thing he said to me was, "I thought only big shots on the East Coast wore bow ties." I laughed. But I knew we would not be friends.

"We're here," said Adams, as chair, "not in a meeting, for as you know that would violate Nebraska law making every meeting of our board an open one, unless personnel matters are on the agenda. And for personnel meetings, at least three days' public notice is required except in emergencies."

"If this is not a meeting," said Anchor, "what the hell is it?"

"It's an informal discussion with President Rosen about his situation," replied Adams.

"Some situation," said Anchor. "Well, I'll start—with a question. Why the hell, Mr. President, couldn't you find a way to get along with the winningest coach in the history of our university? Why couldn't you just focus on what you know something about—academics on the one hand and finances on the other. We hired you because our academic standards were slipping, and our finances made us nervous. Wasn't there more than enough for you to do in handling those problems without picking fights with the greatest coach Nebraska State has ever known?"

"I've been reflecting hard about my relations with Coach Knowland since his death," I responded. "Let me tell you exactly what has happened since I became president twenty-two months ago. You may know some of this, but I'll repeat it anyway."

For the next three hours, Anchor, Carter, and Tyson played tag team, peppering me with sharp questions and snide asides. I tried to stay cool, but it was a struggle. I'll not give the full transcript here, only some of the highlights—if you could call them that.

I began with the story of rescheduling homecoming on a date other than Yom Kippur and then the clash Knowland and I had about the Nebraska State star player who sold his game tickets in violation of NCAA rules.

"So what?" said Carter. "Knowland certainly did more for the university than you seem to have done. Anyway, what was the big deal about Zazoski selling his tickets?"

I tried to be calm in responding. "An NCAA rule was violated, and the university was obligated to report it. If the university doesn't play by the rules, how can we expect our players to do so?"

"You just don't understand how important football is at Nebraska State," Anchor said sharply as his face reddened. "You never did, and you never will." I knew he was as mad as I was.

I went on to tell the trustees that the next season, Knowland refused to talk with me and handled any exchanges with me and my office via his assistants. "I concluded I had more than enough to do without escalating the fight further with Knowland," I said, "though he had been way out of line in our meeting."

"Then the matter was taken out of my hands, and I had no choice but to act—and act decisively," I said. "As you'll recall, a group of women coaches publicly charged that Knowland had discriminated against them in terms of compensation and against their teams in terms of financing. They threatened to sue Knowland, the university, and me unless the matter was resolved quickly."

"Why didn't you just let Knowland handle the matter?" pressed Anchor.

"Because the suit would be against the university and me, as well as Coach Knowland," I responded.

"But the university is sued all the time. What's one more?" said Carter.

"This would have been a suit charging discrimination against women, and that's the difference. The publicity would have been devastating for the university. We faced not only the coaches' suit but likely action by the NCAA and possibly the federal government for violating Title Nine, which prohibits gender discrimination in college sports."

But it was clear that Anchor, Tyler, and Carter were having none of my responses, or "excuses," as they kept calling them.

I plowed ahead recounting that I felt I had no choice but to step in quickly and ask my general counsel, Norman Oreland, to do a complete analysis comparing support for women coaches and women's teams to support for their male counterparts. Knowland called me immediately—the only time since our angry meeting in my office.

"You have no right to interfere in my department," he said. "I know what's right for Nebraska State athletics. I was here before you came, and I will be here after you are gone." Then he hung up.

"How right he was," quipped Anchor, as I stopped for a minute.

I went on to explain how I stressed to Oreland that he would get no help from Knowland or his staff, but the analysis had to be done. "It was," I said, "and the results were devastating." I tried to let that line hang in the air before I went on.

Oreland found that average coaches' salaries comparing men and women differed by at least 15 percent and in some cases 35 percent. Financing for men's teams and women's teams was similarly unbalanced.

"Yeah," Tyler said, "but the newspaper story I read said the unfair treatment of women coaches and their teams was due to 'staff errors in recordkeeping.' And it said Coach Knowland would handle the matter."

"And that's just what should have happened," Anchor interjected. "Why didn't you let him do his job? You never gave Coach Knowland a chance to straighten things out."

"No," I said as calmly as I could, "I felt I had to act quickly and told the women coaches that we were going to hire a new associate director to be in charge of women's teams, and that person would have full authority over their budgets."

At this point, Carter, interrupted. "Yes, and I know Coach Knowland was furious. He told me, 'That son of a bitch will regret trying to screw me.'" Carter added, "And he was absolutely right. I could never run my Ford dealership if I overruled my salesmen whenever they made decisions."

At that point, I just blew up. "Really, Mr. Carter? And what if your salesmen decided to give all their friends discounts? To throw in free extras? To come in late? Even to steal from you? Wouldn't you fire those guys, or at least be sure they never did it again? What Coach Knowland did was not some high school prank like smoking behind the bleachers. He broke the law and violated the university's trust that he would treat men's and women's teams the same."

"Everything you did was just throwing fuel on the fire," snapped Anchor. "You should have just told Coach Knowland to resolve the matter and let him do so."

I didn't have to respond that I couldn't do that, but all the trustees knew that was what I was thinking. I then reminded the trustees that the women coaches chose Frances Juarez, coach of the women's soccer team. I was pleased by their choice because she was the first woman of color to be chosen as associate director in our conference. She is a very tall, stunningly attractive woman, with shining, long black hair and a radiant smile.

"She told me her personal story when we first met shortly after the women coaches chose her," I quickly went on before I was interrupted, to stress that her story was a powerful tribute to her talents and grit. I explained that her parents migrated from Mexico just before she was born, speaking only a few words of English. They were allowed to do so because her mother's sister lived here and sponsored them. They came to Chicago, where her mother was a maid in a Hilton hotel and her father a night watchman in a downtown mall. Neither of her parents had more than a sixth-grade education.

She went on to say that after school and on weekends, she worked throughout high school as a grocery store clerk and then won an athletic scholarship to Northwestern University. She had learned to play basketball first on the Chicago streets and then in school, where her team won the Illinois State championship, and she was voted the most valuable player of the championship. "The fact that I am six-feet-one-inches tall, fast, and a good shot," she told me, "got me the scholarship."

I explained to the trustees that I was blown away by her evident commitment to her players and their welfare. "She obviously loved to win, but the growth and success of students who were also athletes was obviously her primary concern."

"But her appointment ended in disaster," said Carter, "and you didn't see it coming."

"You're right," I admitted. "For the initial months in her role, Juarez seemed to handle well the issues she was facing, though Knowland refused even to talk to her, just as he wouldn't talk with me. Then one day in early June, I received an email from her saying she was resigning her position as associate athletic director, effective immediately. I wrote back immediately and asked Juarez to come to my office. In less than ten minutes, she was there."

The trustees knew what happened, but I thought it important to tell the whole story. "It's embarrassing," she began, "but it would be worse if I did not tell you." I was silent but motioned her to go on.

She told me she was a lesbian and from the outset received ugly anonymous messages calling her filthy names. She had a rough time with a small group of male coaches of women's teams who made it clear they wouldn't take orders from a woman, let alone a gay one. But she stood her ground and was adamant that her support of those coaches and their teams required them to support her. And that worked in terms of her dealings with most of them. Over the first year, she said, she earned their grudging support, if not the enthusiastic approval of all the coaches.

I responded that everything I had heard was positive. I had checked with the women coaches who had threatened to sue, and they seemed really pleased with her leadership. As I told the trustees, those coaches said they were used to Knowland, who was tyrannical in his dealings with all but a few of the coaches. He had a couple of favorites to whom he gave special funding without regard to need. In the performance reviews that Juarez did with the coaches at the end of her first year, they all told her it was the first time they had ever had such a review.

"Then I made a serious mistake," she said. She became good friends with the women's softball coach, Debbie Marlin, and over time their friendship turned into an affair. It was no excuse, she admitted, but she had left all her friends in Madison when she came to Nebraska State from the University of Wisconsin and was lonely. As she put it, "My loneliness turned into what I thought was love—what we both thought was love. We knew that it was wrong for me to have an affair with a subordinate. The university rules are clear about that, though we did not need the rule book to tell us. But Debbie loves being softball coach and does a terrific job. So leaving her job would be really tough for her. And it will be no less tough for me."

She explained that for her to leave after a year would make it almost impossible to find another position. And she was a role model, not only because she was one of the few women associate athletic directors in Division I programs, but also because she was a young Chicana woman.

"The matter was decided for us," she continued, "when I received a call from the male coach of the women's rowing team. He told me he knew about my affair with Debbie and, in exchange for his silence, demanded both increased funding for his rowers and a substantial raise in compensation for himself. I faced an agonizing choice: to accept his terms or leave the job that I love. For a day, I just cried."

Then she went to Debbie and told her she had to step down as associate athletic director. She wryly added that the only satisfaction in doing so was that she would get to report the rowing coach to the police for blackmail.

I asked Juarez what she would do now. In her words, she said, "Debbie and I both hope we can maintain our relationship, but we are realistic enough to know that will be tough. I have to be completely honest with any other campus that might consider hiring me—I made a serious mistake by letting my personal life collide with my responsibilities as associate athletic director." Juarez stressed that it made sense for her to say this publicly then, rather than let the affair slowly leak out in the media. "At least I can craft a statement explaining honestly why I am resigning and wishing the university and its Athletic Department well."

I was stunned, I told the trustees. Over the past years at Nebraska State, I explained, I learned about several affairs in the past between male bosses and their female subordinates. Not one of them had offered to resign. Instead, when the facts leaked out, the women were most often shifted to other departments, and in one case, the woman involved was fired on what in retrospect seemed to me a trumped-up charge. Here was an able and accomplished woman taking responsibility for her mistake and paying a heavy price in doing so.

The trustees knew that Juarez then wrote a public statement explaining in full her affair with Debbie Marlin and her realization that she had violated the university's rules and had to bear full responsibility. The statement told how much she cared for Nebraska State and its Athletic Department and how deeply she regretted that she had to leave. She told everything except about the call from the rowing coach. That story came out when he was charged with blackmail. He negotiated a plea bargain with the local district attorney and was in prison for eighteen months of a three-year sentence. He was also barred from coaching again.

It was a mess, I admitted to the trustees, and the one bit of good news that came from the mess was that Juarez soon was hired as athletic director at a small liberal arts college in Los Angeles, and Martin found a job coaching softball at another university in the area. They were married soon afterward.

I debated whether I should tell the trustees what I had heard about Knowland's reaction and decided to do so. I had given a full report up to then and should continue. As soon as Juarez resigned, I told the trustees, I heard from Robert MacGruder, the chair of the Faculty Athletic Committee, that Knowland was triumphant. "I told you she was a dyke. I'm sure she made passes at our students as well as coaches," he told one of the other coaches, who repeated the comment to MacGruder.

"The newspaper stories that I read about this fiasco," Carter said, "were clear that it never would have happened if you had not undercut Knowland's authority."

I knew it would be useless to respond. Instead, I said that I had restrained myself from any public comments about Knowland until he went one step too far, and the reputation of the whole university was at stake.

"You'll certainly remember," I began, "when Knowland's remarks to a TV commentator, Laura Langley, caused an explosion on the campus and across the country."

Knowland was being interviewed by Langley and was asked about a case that had roiled across the campus the week before. Two football players were accused by a female student of bringing her to their room, giving her vodka drinks until she passed out, and then raping her. The student said she remembered nothing after the third drink but was so sore after the two players dropped her off in front of her dorm that she checked into the campus health center, was tested, and learned she had been raped. The two football players both swore that the female student was not only willing to have sex with them but actively encouraged them.

The female student brought charges against the two, and the case was being heard by the campus commission on sexual harassment at the time Knowland was being interviewed. When asked by Langley what he thought of the situation, Knowland replied, "I don't know exactly what happened, but I do know that no girl should go to a guy's dorm room and not expect something like that."

I opened my laptop and played for the trustees the video clip of Knowland saying those words to Laura Langely. It was shown on the nightly news and covered in newspapers across the country, and I heard the story almost immediately. I told the trustees I tried to reach Knowland by phone, but his assistants all claimed he was nowhere to be found.

The trustees knew I had issued a press release and appeared on a CBS news report. "Coach Knowland's responses to Ms. Langely were totally offensive," I said, "and in no way represent the values of Nebraska State University. All members of the university community have a responsibility to treat everyone with dignity and respect. Coach Knowland failed to carry out that responsibility. His comments disgraced the whole university."

None of the trustees defended Knowland's comments, but Tyler said I should have waited to comment until I had talked to Knowland, ignoring that I had just made clear I had tried and failed because Knowland was nowhere to be found.

"He went into hiding," I added. "MacGruder had ties to most of the football coaching staff. He told me that Knowland was furious at being snookered by a woman, Laura Langely, and mad at his two accused players. So he lashed out at me, telling reporters that I had never supported him the way that my predecessor had and that I had a personal vendetta against him. Word quickly leaked out that he was being courted by Colorado State University. He had a fishing ranch in Colorado, so it was a place that had obvious attractions to him."

As I told the trustees, I had to decide what to do. On the one hand, Knowland was a terrible role model for students, and I would have been delighted to see him go. But on the other hand, I had a university-wide academic agenda underway and feared it would be derailed by the Knowland controversy.

My fear was based on past experiences of other university presidents. One of them, a good friend from Arizona, had announced when he was appointed that no freshmen could play varsity sports, to give them time to get used to campus life and particularly to their academic responsibilities. I thought this made a lot of sense. But three star football recruits decided not to go to Arizona after the new policy was announced. Sports fans in Arizona were immediately up in arms and put so much pressure on the trustees that they forced the president to rescind the rule. Unfortunately, however, for an entire year until that happened, the president could get nothing done because of the controversy.

The trustees knew the rest of the story, but I told it to them anyway. In the week after Knowland's TV interview, the faculty senate approved a resolution 68 to 7 urging me to fire him. But, as I wrote, a large group of students marched to my house on the campus shouting support for Knowland. From across Nebraska and beyond, I received over three thousand emails and letters. Those from inside Nebraska overwhelmingly supported Knowland. The governor even called me. "Do you realize," he said, "how serious this is? You have to find a way to hold onto Knowland. He's more popular than either of us."

"Yes," I responded, "I know that."

Those messages from outside the state were almost uniformly against Knowland. Letters and calls came from across the country calling on me to fire Knowland. Everyone who wrote received a form response with my signature stamped on it. "Thank you for your helpful comments," it said. "The entire university and I appreciate your interest."

The matter was settled, of course, at the end of the week when Knowland died on the field after a massive heart attack. But I knew his spirit was all too alive and well, and I feared what damage that spirit could do.

There I was, sitting in my own office, being cross-examined by the trustees before they would decide my professional fate. When I finished my account of my battles with Knowland, the room was quiet for a moment. Then I spoke again.

"I love Nebraska State," I said, "and I love being president because of the opportunities to help make a great university even greater. You hired me to do just that. I've made a start. But I am not finished. I hope you will allow me to continue."

I might have gone on, but Adams broke in and asked me to step outside so that the trustees could "discuss the matter."

"The matter," of course, was me.

3

The red and yellow leaves floated softly in the breeze before carpeting the ground. Students carrying backpacks and computers rushed and biked and laughed and greeted friends as they made their way through the Rossiter Quad. Some were tossing footballs on the lawn, while others were having picnics on the grass. Sandstone buildings dating to the founding of Nebraska State dominated the quad.

It was a crisp, beautiful fall day in Nebraska as I sat looking out a window in an anteroom outside my office, waiting to be called back to hear the trustees' verdict. The fact that the board chair, Adams, called me "President Rosen," instead of "Charlie," as he had since my appointment, intensified my anxiety.

The postcard-perfect weather belied the butterflies in my stomach. I wondered whether the ax would fall, thinking, "Why is it that dealing with intercollegiate athletics is the least favorite part of my job, when I've enjoyed sports so much for most of my life?" I relished watching most sports and still played tennis doubles when I got the chance. And I made a point to keep up with the university's teams in every sport. There was a tingling sense of excitement for me in seeing intercollegiate competition. *Especially* football.

Football. I loved it. I also hated it.

I loved football because it made fans throughout Nebraska and beyond feel they were part of the university when they are rooting for our team. Every home game was a festival, gayer and greater even than commencements. Games were always on a Saturday, but festivities started on Thursday, when fans from hundreds of miles away trickled into town, many in RVs, and started tailgating. By Friday afternoon, the huge parking lot that circles the stadium was jammed with every kind of vehicle. "Blazing blue" was the Nebraska State color, and from the air the stadium looked like a blue ocean. Fans wore blue hats, blue shirts, and blue pants; some even painted their faces blue.

The fans drank beer, sang the team fight song, barbecued on portable grills, and partied. Whatever the problems in their lives, this was a time to have fun and not to worry about anything other than whether our team won the game. For most, even that was not so important as long as they had a good time and were with their friends.

Our fans filled the stadium for every game, unlike four of the seven campuses in our conference that had losing seasons for years, with the result that their stadiums were usually less than half full. Winning brought fans, and for that—much as I hated to say it—I had to give credit to Knowland and his winning ways. Because of him, our football program carried the other sports programs within the university. Men's basketball was the only other program that might have more than broken even, but our team hadn't come close to a conference championship in more than a decade. Women's basketball, on the other hand, had brought us several championships, though its fan base was not strong enough to earn a surplus.

Our fans relied on the football games for their amusement, but a huge web of local folks relied on the games for their incomes. The hotels and motels within a hundred miles of the campus doubled their rates on game weekends, and they were booked solid. Food vendors with colorful personalities and booming voices trekked up and down the stadium stairs, yelling, "Get your popcorn! Get your peanuts!"—just as they did at pro games. Then there were the hamburgers, the hot dogs, the programs, the souvenirs, and, of course, the five-dollar cups filled with a dollar's worth of beer. Scores of cooks and cashiers served fast food to hungry fans at outrageous prices. Security guards patrolled the stadium, watching for pickpockets and keeping the drunks in line.

Game time depended on when the event was to be televised. But whenever that was, the stadium began to fill up with fans about two hours before kickoff. For most games, only a small section was reserved for fans of the opposing team. (The "Big Game" against the University of Nebraska—the one when Knowland died on the field—was an exception because its fans were allowed to purchase almost one-third of the tickets.)

The band was there beforehand, playing and marching up and down the field, literally drumming up excitement, but leaving plenty of room for players from both teams to come onto the field for last-minute drills and warm-ups. Usually, a few players from past championship teams also came onto the field and were introduced by the announcer to cheers from the fans.

"I wonder how many times their wives have had to listen to the same story about the winning touchdown," Emma said to me under her breath as the old-timers waved to the crowd. No surprise, the three trustees who played for Knowland had been honored this way on multiple occasions.

A few minutes before game time, the players went back to the locker rooms, and the band played the university alma mater song. The fans stood up, and some tried to sing it, but it was a terrible tune, and the words were forgettable. "Stand for old N State, where so many met their mate," is one line I recall. Most fans just used the time to stretch. Then everyone remained standing, and the band played "The Star-Spangled Banner," while a student singer from our music school belted the song. American pride and good manners meant more here than being on key, and everyone gave an enthusiastic standing ovation at the end—as if we just had heard Whitney Houston. Most fans knew these words and sang along, especially at the end, when all Americans cheered like crazy: "Oh say does that star-spangled banner yet wave? O'er the land of the free and the home of the brave." The roars went on when the captains of the two teams came to the middle of the field and a referee tossed a coin. One captain called heads or tails, and the winner chose whether to begin the game playing offense or defense, while the other captain chose at which end of the stadium his team would start. And the game began!

Meanwhile, Emma and I were in the President's Sky Box, a large glass-enclosed affair suspended over one side of the playing field and held there by huge beams clamped to the stadium. A giant, blue Nebraska State banner hung on the back wall, behind a bar that ran the length of the box. Three servers were always on duty at the bar to provide free food and drinks. Everyone coming into the box was given a souvenir blue pin to wear on their jackets. Looking down at the fans from the box, the inside of the stadium was a sea of blue.

The President's Sky Box holds thirty-two persons, and I used it at every home game to entertain about a dozen top donors and their spouses. These were so-called cultivation events, not times to ask for money. Sprinkled among the donors were some deans and development staff to be sure the donors were well taken care of and that they knew key facts about the university's financial needs. A changing group of carefully selected faculty and students was also chosen to sit in the box for each game, always next to a donor. Ideally, they came from the towns where the donors lived and were briefed on the background of the donors they would sit with as well as their past and potential interests in gifts to the university. Finally, two seats were always reserved for fans from the local community who had won the "Presidential Sky Box lottery." They had their picture taken with me during the game, and the picture usually appeared the next day in the community newspaper.

Most people I knew hated to ask for money and to do the things that went along with asking. But Emma and I both enjoyed fundraising. Most of the donors and potential donors with whom we talked were interesting people, and their stories were often fascinating—how they got to where they were. A key, we found, was to be sure to shape a request for contributions to the donors' interests while being equally sure that the request aligned with the university's needs. The other essential was not to take it personally when a donor refused.

Emma and I usually invited one or two of the most important donors to dinner at our home on Friday night, and then they stayed over as our guests. This was prime time in terms of my pitching a special program or project that needed financial support, one to which we would add the donor's name.

Once a football game was underway, every time our team made a good play, our fans screamed, the band played, fireworks went off, and an enormous horn blared. Fans booed when they thought the referees made a bad call and cheered when the opposing team fumbled or made a bad play.

Often, when I was watching a game, I wondered what would happen to most of the players—they were just kids after all. I worried about all the players, even those who didn't get hurt. They practiced at least six hours a day during the season and worked out year-round lifting weights and running sprints. Most players on the first team aspired to play in the NFL, though rarely more than one or two of our players made that leap. Our Nebraska State teams usually had at least 100 players, though NCAA rules limited those who received scholarships to 85. Of course far fewer played in a game except for the last few minutes if our team was several touchdowns ahead. I've never understood why the NCAA allowed more than the 53 players the NFL permits on a team.

Most fans came away feeling good about Nebraska State, no matter which team won. It was their university, whether or not they had been students here. The games renewed and strengthened their bonds to the university.

So why did I hate football, as well as love it? Because it was literally a killer. The facts were chilling. You probably know them. Some players died from their injuries. Many more were maimed for life. Torn shoulders, back and spine injuries, and more—football could cripple players for life. The worst were the concussions caused by the brain bouncing around in the skull, like a racquetball bouncing over and over against the walls of an enclosed court, leading to traumatic brain injury (CTE). The *Journal of the American Medical Association* reported that CTE caused by concussions was found in 91 percent of college football players. And CTE had been shown to lead to suicidal and violent behavior and dementia.

Most of the concussions and other injuries happened during practices rather than the games, though those in games were the only ones the fans see. These injuries were not all Knowland's fault, I realized. But according to his reputation, he drove his players harder than any other coach in our conference. Knowland screamed at them whenever a block or tackle was not as hard as he wanted. "Candy asses!" he'd call these players. And he rewarded players with star stickers pasted to their helmets whenever they "smashed" an opposing player particularly well. The players with the most stars at the end of the season received awards.

Did the players at least get a decent education in return? I feared many, perhaps most, did not. They received intensive academic support from special tutors, most majored in a soft field at Nebraska State like communications, and most also took a light academic load during the fall and graduated—if at all—in five or six years.

Some of the star players were hired in the summer by local automobile dealers, who paid them well for little work. It was a violation of NCAA rules for coaches to arrange these gigs, but I heard rumors that Knowland did just that.

Slowly, in my time as president, I came to realize that I hated football because it was driving a dangerous wedge, fueled by money, between the academic arena, which should be primary at any university, and intercollegiate athletics, which had taken primacy at too many universities. Externally, those Division I campuses were known primarily for their football teams, the highest-salaried employees were the football coaches, many players were there as a gateway to the NFL, the alumni's concern was only the football team, and the quality of the academic arena was overshadowed by football. This sad state of affairs seemed to me true at the University of Nebraska, and I had challenged myself not to let that happen at Nebraska State. I was not sure I was up to the challenge.

Something else caused me to hate football after I became president. That something else, of course, was Knowland. His behavior took much of the joy out of the game for me. He was gone, yet I didn't know whether I could go back to watching football games with pleasure. Or would the ghost of Knowland forever cast its shadow and preclude that pleasure?

Watching other sports was a joy for me. Each year I made it a priority to attend at least one game or match played by every varsity team, which means watching at least twenty-two events; nine men's games and thirteen women's. When it was a team sport, I sat on the bench and had a chance to talk to players and coaches during a game.

Because the athletic director reported directly to the president at Nebraska State, like all other universities in our conference, I seemed to be ensnared in the problem whenever there was trouble involving one of our coaches or teams. And then I was usually asked by a reporter what I was going to do to solve the problem. I quickly learned that it was not helpful to say, "That's an issue for our athletic director." The inquiring reporter would then report, "President Rosen refused to answer the question." Our local newspaper had a terrific political cartoonist who loved to show me with a tennis racket in one hand trying to cover my face from seeing some screw-up in athletics.

During the two and a half years since I had become president, I had received literally thousands of letters and emails from alumni. Most wrote just to say how supportive they were of their alma mater, and even if they did not attend Nebraska State, they often called it "their university." When they wrote, many mentioned that their kids or other relatives graduated from the main campus or one of the two regional campuses, which spoke to how much they wanted to be part of this tribe.

I also regularly received plenty of letters of complaint, and most often they were about some perceived failure in Nebraska State athletics. I didn't love the vitriol that too often came my way with those letters. I kept one letter framed on the wall of my office to remind me not to let my head get too big as president: "I'm eighty-eight years old, stuck in a wheelchair, and I live for Nebraska State football. You can take your Goddamn bow ties and go back to banking, where you belong." As I said, the only ties I wore were bow ties. And I wore them regularly as a banker before switching to teaching.

"Why stake your career as an athletic director on the physical prowess of eighteen-year-old kids?" I often muttered to myself. Being a coach was tough enough. But at least you had a chance to work directly with kids, so they could display and enhance their talents. Especially as the coach of a team sport, you were able to help your players understand the value of teamwork, a lesson that can last a lifetime. I'm sure working with players was why Knowland insisted on staying on as football coach after being chosen as athletic director. In that dual role, he had an obvious conflict of interest when the interests of the football program clashed with the interests of the other sports. Knowland always came down on the side of football.

Insofar as I could tell, being an athletic director offered nothing but heartaches. You were in charge of a group of one-note, ego-intensive coaches, each of whom thought her or his sport was the most important. You could help build strong teams by hiring the right coaches, but all too often you had to fire them when their teams were losing.

Having a strong fan base was key to avoiding losing too much money in intercollegiate athletics. Though my predecessors and I had been generally successful in hiding this reality from the campus community and the public, intercollegiate athletics at the university lost over a million dollars a year. The deficit would have been worse, of course, without football. Our revenues from football were a fraction of the University of Nebraska's, however, especially after that campus joined the Big Ten Conference.

Since I became president of Nebraska State University, I'd always been irritated that the University of Nebraska at Lincoln was too often viewed in our state as the powerhouse in academics as well as athletics. (The University of Nebraska had four campuses, and the one in Lincoln was the flagship.) By every measure, my university was stronger in academic terms. We attracted more research dollars (largely from our medical school), and we had more highly ranked academic departments, more faculty who had been elected to prestigious national academies, and more students who had won Rhodes and other national and international scholarships. Yet neither my predecessors nor I had made any progress in persuading the Nebraska legislature that our state funding per student should be at least equal to that of the Cornhuskers.

Here's another reason I was jealous of the University of Nebraska and unhappy because of the unfair preferences it received. The American Association of Universities, called the AAU, was the most academically prestigious organization of universities in the country. It had sixty-three members, chosen on the basis of their research strength. The Big Ten Conference long prided itself on including only members of that association. The University of Nebraska was an AAU member when it joined the Big Ten. Ironically, the next year the University of Nebraska was thrown out of the AAU because it lacked research strength. When that happened, I pressed for my university to be invited to join. Privately, other presidents whose campuses were members told me Nebraska State University was entitled to join based on our research strength, but they could not go ahead because that would be seen as a slap in the face of the University of Nebraska. To me, that illogic was absurd, and I was furious. At the same time, as I told my staff regularly, we had adopted the old ad slogan of Avis Rent-a-Car when comparing itself to Hertz: "We try harder."

Nebraska State was part of the Big Seven, a seven-university conference of Division I universities—the top athletic division. The presidents in the conference met twice a year, and it was through the other presidents that I began to get an education in big-time intercollegiate athletics. The Big Seven universities stretched across the Midwest and the Rockies, and there was never-ending pressure to add more universities with large numbers of fans, because that would translate into greater TV revenues. Televised football and basketball games supported more than half the costs of all our athletic programs through advertising dollars.

The advice I gained from the other conference presidents was not limited to athletics. I could still hear one of my favorites, Caroline Conway from Wyoming State University, say to me in a battle-weary voice, "As president, you can only tackle two, or at most three, big issues at any one time. You need to be prepared that one of those issues will not be a priority on your agenda but rather a priority for some group that you need to keep happy. Something unseen can come up and ruin your presidency unless you are on top of it immediately and in a proactive way."

Conway recounted a story I had already heard before about a former conference president, Wayne Henning, a decade earlier. Henning's wife decided to renovate a former mansion given by a wealthy university alumnus and transform the mansion into a university conference center. The total cost was over one million dollars, which might seem reasonable given the grandeur of the home. But for months, the press focused solely on what a million dollars could support in terms of student scholarships. The president should have said, "I made a mistake, and I will not make that error again. I appreciate the frank way in which members of our community made that clear to me. I'm committed to correcting my mistake by raising the costs of renovation entirely from a few supporters of the university who have been eager for us to have a first-rate conference center."

Instead, Henning kept defending the action, no doubt in part because in doing so he was also defending his wife. After almost a year of public harassment on the matter, Henning resigned, even though his agenda was largely left undone.

"If you want reforming athletics to be one of your key successes in your presidency, that's fine," Conway told me. "And good luck, because there is no bundle of issues on which alumni are more passionate. But try not to let yourself get sucked into a battle that is not of your choosing." As I would quickly find out, that was sage advice.

In my first year as president, I had to approve halting ice hockey as an intercollegiate sport at the same time we added women's field hockey. Ice hockey was expensive because of the need to keep up an intercollegiate ice rink. I would not have thought ice hockey was a big deal in Nebraska, but it turned out it was for those who had played it at the university. I heard a torrent of complaints, including an anonymous phone message promising to push a hockey stick up my rear end. An alumni fund was started to "save" ice hockey, and under pressure from two trustees, as well as alumni, I committed to re-instituting the sport if adequate funds were raised. After some months, the protest finally fizzled. Alumni raised only a few thousand dollars, which was eventually returned to the donors.

So, as I've said, unlike hockey, football was the big deal at Nebraska State. Our football team had won twice as many games as it had lost since I became president, but it had never been ranked in the top tier of teams nationally. The team went to two bowl games in that time, but neither was a major bowl. I learned only after the first bowl game that, except for a few major bowl games, it cost more to send the team, the coaches, the band, and cheerleaders to play in a bowl game than the university received in revenue. And it would have been heresy to have suggested that the football team play without the band and the cheerleaders there to support it.

Men's basketball could also have brought a celebratory spirit, as well as revenue, but our team was consistently ranked at the bottom of our conference. We had only two teams that were among the best in the nation: women's soccer and men's diving. Each had a remarkable coach who had been at the university for over a decade and had made those teams preeminent. Their coaches impressed me not only because their teams rarely lost but also because they seldom yelled at their players—or anyone else. Rather, they were mild-mannered and polite, to the press and to everyone else. What a contrast with most of the other coaches, especially Knowland!

I didn't know until I became president that part of the job was being constantly harassed by alumni who had been members of a university team and felt that team was being shortchanged in some way. I received most of the blame, even though I left decisions about allocating athletic resources and athletic scholarships entirely in the hands of the Athletic Department.

The only major exception to my "hands off" policy was when the FBI caught and the US attorney's office indicted our fencing coach for accepting bribes for the fencing team—not for himself—from a wealthy Omaha businessman in exchange for telling the admissions office that the businessman's son was a star fencer. The kid had not even picked up a fencing foil until the week before he applied. Recently, of course, such misdeeds became national news, but I guessed they had been going on at some universities, particularly elite ones, for years.

I had to bring in an outside law firm to determine whether there might have been other similar misdeeds by other coaches and then put a review of oversight of all athletic scholarships in the hands of Norman Oreland, to the irritation of Knowland.

"Keep your damn lawyers off my football field," he yelled at me when he learned about that step.

"No way," I yelled back, "not when the university is getting cheated." This was one more clash in our ongoing battle.

That scandal did not stop alumni from claiming that I was really making the decisions and that I personally failed to allocate enough athletic scholarships to their teams or that those teams were underfunded. Being in the same state as an athletic powerhouse, the University of Nebraska, meant that the coaches, the athletic director, and I were always hearing unfavorable comparisons.

Intercollegiate athletics was also its own form of hell for any university and its president because the NCAA rule book was bigger and more complicated than the IRS tax regulations. Whenever the NCAA would adopt a new rule, coaches would find a loophole to get around the rule. Then a new rule would be adopted to plug the evasion. And almost immediately a new work-around would be found. For example, videos of high school athletes became common practice when coaches' visits to watch the kids play were restricted. Similarly, when the NCAA limited the numbers of coaches' visits to the homes of high school students, coaches started having virtual calls with prospective players.

Complaints about sexual harassment began exploding all over the university, especially in the Athletic Department, about a decade before I became president, and the quantity of cases grew steadily each year. I never knew for sure whether this was because the number of sexual misdeeds was increasing or rather that women students were gradually more willing to register complaints. I suspect both were happening.

For two years, we had a conference champion women's golf team, but over Knowland's objections, we had to fire the male coach when a couple of team members complained that he told them their "butts and breasts were too big." Further, when Robert MacGruder, the head of the Faculty Athletic Committee, told me when we were watching a tennis match together soon after I became president that Knowland boasted he never hired women coaches for women's teams because most of the applicants were lesbians. I sent word via MacGruder (without ever putting this in writing) that the next vacancy in coaching a women's team must be a woman, though he had to interview both women and men for the job. MacGruder said Knowland growled but complied.

After two hours of sitting outside in the quad and contemplating all this and more in my anxious mind, I returned to my office to wait for the trustees' verdict. I continued replaying in my mind my bouts with Knowland until, finally, Adams came out of the conference room and asked me to return. When I sat down at one end of the table facing all the trustees, Adams looked at me and said, "We've had an informal discussion, and we've decided to give you another chance. Frankly, I have to admit that not all my colleagues were in favor of this step. With their concerns in mind, the trustees have decided to give you six months to find a superb new athletic director, one whom the board can unanimously support to lead our Athletic Department to new heights in intercollegiate sports. And one more thing: we insist that the new athletic director also be the new football coach, one who can lead the team to victories, just as Coach Knowland did. Some of the trustees believe we will be able to attract a much stronger candidate if the jobs stay combined, as they were under Coach Knowland."

I was stunned for a minute. Then I responded, "What you propose makes no sense to me. For one thing, combining the jobs of athletic director and football coach creates a blatant conflict of interest, as Coach Knowland's behavior made clear. He did what anyone in both jobs would do—favored football at the expense of other sports."

"Well," responded Adams, "the trustees think Coach Knowland did a fine job for Nebraska State athletics and was a great football coach, as well. We are very pleased we chose him for both jobs."

Knowing it was useless to argue that issue further, I pressed on in a different direction. "Searches often take much longer than six months," I said, "if they are to succeed, and I'm sure you want a search that is successful."

"We know that," Adams said, "but that is all the time you have to get the job done. Speaking personally, Charlie, I believe you can do it." I noted that this time he called me Charlie, unlike when he ushered me out of my office to await the trustees' decision, as if this might soften the blow.

I must have looked a bit dazed as the trustees left my office. Adams stayed behind. "As must be clear to you, Charlie," he told me, "this is not what I wanted, but it was the best deal I could get. I hope you can live with it. I will understand if you just decide to resign, though I very much hope you will not. You have been a fine president, apart from your clashes with Knowland, and I have great confidence that in future years, if you stay, you will be known as one of our university's greatest presidents."

In a daze tinged with fury, I walked slowly back to the president's house, located just ten minutes away, right in the middle of the campus. Emma was waiting for me, and I quickly told her the news.

"Those bastards!" I exploded. "Adams—the guy mainly responsible for choosing me—claims he stood up for me. I wonder how much of a fight he really made for me. They expect me to organize a search for some kind of miracle man who can be both athletic director and football coach, which is a ridiculous combination, as Knowland proved all too well."

"Don't yell at me," Emma said quietly. "And stop your temper tantrum, as you promised me before we married. You can just say no. They'll fire you, and under your contract, we will have two and a half years for you to find another job. But you shouldn't be surprised. Remember, the trustees are the ones who agreed that Knowland could have both jobs over Enrico's objection. And Enrico quit. But you're not a quitter. Why not try to find someone who can do both jobs in a way that makes sense to you? And if you can't, you can walk away knowing at least you tried. If you leave the job now, you'll also leave the university in a mess, and all the initiatives you've started will fail. You can be angry all night. But my vote is that you start the search process tomorrow."

It took me awhile, but within a few hours, I realized Emma was right. I should do my best to select a new athletic director / football coach who represented the values I care about, along with having the skills needed for the job. If in six months I failed, at least I would never regret not trying.

Lots of questions were swirling around in my mind. We would need a search committee with representatives from all relevant constituencies, for established university rules required that. But who would be on the committee? Who would chair the committee? Perhaps most troublesome, should I reveal that the trustees had mandated that the new athletic director must also be the football coach? And should I make clear that I would be fired if a successful search was not concluded in just six months?

Emma and I went to sleep with those and many other questions unresolved. But we both knew that the next six months would be an intense roller coaster of challenges. And we realized even then that we could not let the search hobble my ability to lead a full agenda of activities that needed to be done to strengthen the university—apart from athletics.

At this point, I had best explain my background, how I was chosen for the job of president, and something of what that job entails. My credentials as president were unusual because I did not have a traditional academic career, but that seemed to be what the trustees wanted. I had grown up in New Haven, where my mother was a public high school teacher, and my father owned a small pipe and tobacco store—long before we knew the dangers of smoking. As I have said, my father was an abusive bully when he was drunk. That was virtually every Saturday and Sunday night and many weekday evenings as well. If bad tempers are a matter of genes, I know where mine came from.

I went to the school where my mother taught and won a scholarship to Yale, where I majored in economics. On graduation, I was hired by Goldman Sachs in New York. After six years, although I had become a partner, I'd had more than enough of the dog-eat-dog New York world of investment banking and wanted to head a bank in a suburb or perhaps a small town where I didn't have to screw my customers and colleagues for money. With the help of a search firm, I was hired to be president of Catherville Bank in Catherville, Nebraska. The bank has branches throughout the greater Catherville area. In honor of Nebraska's most famous writer, the name of the town had been changed to Catherville when Willa Cather died in 1947.

I met Emma on the main campus of Nebraska State in Catherville, where the university art gallery was having a show of her paintings and those of three other women artists. Emma was not beautiful in a traditional sense. But her face was striking. She broke her nose as a teenager playing soccer, and it never completely straightened. Her most prominent feature was her intense blue eyes, which seemed to signal she knew exactly what I was thinking even before I spoke a word. Her light brown hair was cut at the shoulders, and she was about five feet four inches.

Emma was an accomplished painter at the time, though her full-time job was working at an art supply store near the university. While at the store, she earned an MFA at the University of Nebraska. I was intrigued by her art, which included a beautiful series of Nebraska landscapes as well as a number of abstract paintings. I found out her name and phone number from the gallery, called, and asked if we could meet for coffee. I fell in love that first date, though it took her a bit longer. We dated for just a year before we were married. When our twins were born, she stopped working at the store and spent most of her time taking care of our twins and working on her painting. She's had two shows in a Lincoln art gallery and has sold a number of her pictures. And she became an adjunct professor of art at Nebraska State, teaching a range of classes on painting, for beginners to advanced students.

Emma enabled me to become a feminist. It is not that I didn't think women should have equal rights as an abstract matter. But working at Goldman Sachs and then at my bank, I never stopped to examine the gender discrimination that was ongoing at both places. Yes, both had women officers, but with Emma's guidance I came to see that women were at a real disadvantage in terms of hiring and promotion. There was nothing I could do about changing the Goldman Sachs culture, but that was exactly what I did at the bank. We appointed our first female vice president, soon added three women as head of bank branches, and then two women to our board of directors.

Emma was a complicated woman, like all interesting people. She had many admirable characteristics, and the one I liked the most was her curiosity. I often said that she had never seen a door or drawer that she did not want to open. She also had the rare ability to find something interesting in almost everyone. And she had a fantastic memory for the names of people and the details about their families. When she walked into a room full of Nebraska State alumni, she seemed to know everyone and everything about their children and grandchildren.

Emma had strong views on many things. She disliked most intercollegiate sports, and football particularly. She hid it well when we were with others. But when we were alone, she would unload about the ways she thought our football players were treated like professional prize fighters for whom education was a side show. Of course, Knowland's misbehavior just stoked her fire on the subject. Even after he died, she would have cheered if Nebraska State gave up football, though she knew that was not going to happen.

Emma and I did many activities together, which I loved. But appearing at various games and matches to cheer Nebraska State teams was not one of them. Football was different because we had the President's Sky Box, and she would spend time during games talking with donors and prospective donors. She was masterful at that. She could find just the right topic that interested a deep-pocketed guest of ours in the Sky Box and engage that person about the topic as though it were of special interest to her. And she was not faking. She was eager to learn about almost anything. She was intensely curious as well as extremely sociable. These qualities made her the perfect person with whom to have a conversation.

Apart from football, however, we had a pact that while I would often ask her to join me at campus events, sports would never be involved. "God gave us two legs for hiking," she used to tell me, "and that is not only exercise enough for me; it is what I love to do."

Our twins, Amy and Abby, were not identical and had very different personalities, though they were the closest of friends. Abby took after Emma, and Amy after me. Both were mercurial, adolescent girls, but Abby had a kind or dreamy, artistic temperament, while Amy was quick to laugh and quick to anger. They loved acting together and were in every school play. They were also musicians—Abby played the violin, and Amy the cello. They formed a string quartet at their school and played in the school orchestra.

Girls in their school seemed constantly to be forming cliques, ones that left some girls feeling miserable because they were not included. Both of our girls insisted that any clique had to include them both, or neither would join. They often squabbled at home, but everywhere else they were an inseparable team.

My family life fitted well with my work at the bank. By the end of my first year, when I did an extensive reorganization, the work was not particularly taxing. After a while it became so routine that I was often bored. But the job gave me time to be home every day for dinner and to study at night for an MBA at Nebraska State on the Catherville campus. After a couple of years, I started teaching banking at Nebraska State as an adjunct professor. When I could not find a textbook on the basics of banking I liked, I wrote my own. Over time, I found I enjoyed teaching and writing more than being a banker. For me, it beat grappling with the financial needs of farmers and businesspeople around Nebraska.

I left the bank after eight years to accept the deanship of the Nebraska State University Business School. The appointment was controversial because I was not an academic, and the faculty was deeply suspicious whether I could understand that the school was not just another business but rather a place for scholarship and teaching. I had an MBA, not a PhD. I had written a book, but it was a textbook, not a scholarly one.

Over my five years as dean, I gradually won over most of the business faculty, at least grudgingly. In the first year, I closed a deficit in the Business School's budget that had been slowly draining reserves for much of the past decade. And I almost doubled the school's endowment. I started a leadership circle of businessmen and women who were CEOs of their Nebraska companies. They agreed to fund one to five full scholarships at the school, depending on the size of their businesses. In exchange, though I never said it this way, those leaders were invited to dinners with the students they had supported and, as a result, had an edge in hiring the best students.

There were still a few school faculty who resented me and thought I could never be an effective leader because I did not have a PhD. But the rest of the faculty generally agreed that the school was stronger since I became its leader.

One incident, to my surprise, ended up getting me lots of favorable support in the local media and within the university. It probably also helped in persuading the trustees that I was the right person to be the next president. It involved Jay Jacobs, a friend from our high school days who had defended me before the officers of our college fraternity when I got in a fight with Leonard Lyons and broke his arm in three places.

Jacobs had remained my good friend since we graduated from Nebraska State. We worked together at Goldman Sachs, and when I became Business School dean, I helped persuade him to join the school's faculty. He then wrote a series of academic articles extolling the virtues of credit-default swaps, which is a kind of fancy financial instrument. I only realized this as I was reviewing his dossier for promotion from associate to full professor. I noted the articles and remembered that he had been active in the field while we were both at Goldman Sachs.

On a hunch, I called the CEO of Goldman Sachs and asked him if the firm was paying Jacobs as an adviser on those financial instruments. The CEO said he'd check, and when he called back, he reported that the firm had Jacobs on a six-figure retainer, with the expectation that he would regularly write papers endorsing credit-default swaps. That was enough for me. Jacobs had a clear conflict of interest writing articles praising those financial instruments without revealing he was paid for the articles by Goldman Sachs. I called Jacobs into my office and said he had to resign immediately, or I would start university procedures to fire him.

Jacobs was furious at me. "How could you betray me like this given our lifetime of friendship, particularly when I defended you after your fight at our fraternity? But for my help, you probably would have been expelled from college when the fight became public. And now you turn on me as though I were a stranger."

As calmly as I could, I explained that I had no choice once I learned what Jacobs was doing. He remained furious but agreed to resign, knowing that the alternative would have been even worse for him.

After his sudden departure, word of his misdeeds quickly leaked throughout the university. I had to call an emergency meeting of the business faculty and explain exactly what had happened. The incident ended my friendship with Jacobs, but it helped cement my relationship with the rest of the faculty and with the trustees.

In retrospect, I realize that when I started as dean, I was often brash and unwilling to build a consensus on key moves I wanted to make. It took time for me to come to understand that no one gives orders in a university, as they do in business. Rather, campus leaders have to build trust. Faculty, students, and staff have to gain a real sense that they are part of a community in which they belong. The school's challenges are their challenges, not just the dean's. Otherwise, when they have a problem, they will say, "We have a real crisis. Now you, Mr. Dean, go fix it."

For example, when I started, the Business School was on the semester system while the rest of the university was on the quarter system. I began my first faculty meeting by saying we needed to shift to the quarter system, so we could establish joint-degree programs with the Engineering School and the Law School, along with the Medical School, and perhaps other schools as well. In addition, a shift to the quarter system would enable our students to take courses outside the Business School.

At that first faculty meeting, a majority argued that the semester system was much better for the courses they were teaching. Some even said that if a change had to be made, the university should switch to the semester system, something I knew would never happen. I had to withdraw my proposal and suggest instead that the faculty curriculum committee study the matter and report back the pros and cons of a shift. Meanwhile, I talked informally with every faculty member and made the case for why the change would strengthen the school and its national sanding. It took almost a year, but the process enabled a solid majority to agree that the shift was a wise move.

Over my years as dean, I learned other lessons about leadership, and in the process, I learned about myself, my strengths and weaknesses. My first speech to an alumni group in Lincoln was one I spent a great deal of time polishing and practicing. I thought the text was clear and forceful in explaining the challenges facing the Business School and how I proposed to meet those challenges. I read it several times and thought I could deliver well. At the end of my talk, the president of one of the largest banks in the state and a loyal Nebraska State alumnus came up to me and quietly said, "Charlie, if you can't talk about your school without reading a script, you don't deserve to be dean." He was right, of course, though his words hurt at the time. I never again read a speech.

I also worked to control my temper. But one late afternoon, Polly Porter mixed up my appointment for that evening with another appointment, and I started yelling at her. She came up to me and, just inches in front of my face, said quietly, "If you ever do that again, I'll not only quit but tell the school why I am doing it." I never did that again. She also gave me wise advice that I'll always remember. "Too often," she said, "when you are angry at something that just happened, you yell at staff, whether or not they had anything to do with the matter, knowing they can't yell back. You should honor them with respect, especially when they make a mistake."

I had been dean for five years when I became the university president. My predecessor, Enzo Enrico, had been president for the preceding sixteen years. When he was chosen, he had been vice chancellor for administration at the University of Nebraska. He was selected by the trustees in an emergency meeting when the prior president was forced out because his alcoholism had become too visible. Under Enzo's leadership, the university had been slowly losing both students and prestige, and the board wanted someone with business experience. But the faculty wanted someone with academic experience. Enrico was not an academic, and the faculty groused about that for his entire tenure. I was both an academic—at least sort of—and had business experience. And I had a degree from Nebraska State, which certainly helped with the alumni.

My appointment was controversial because the Faculty Senate had passed a resolution calling on the board to appoint a leading scholar, arguing that only a scholar could understand the strengths of the university and how those strengths could best be enhanced. I was certainly not a leading scholar. A textbook on banking, supplemented by a few articles on issues in the field, was not the scholarly work of discovery in the minds of most faculty members but rather a synthesis of my own thoughts and those of other economists—a summary of knowledge in the field. But a majority of the search committee were trustees, and this was enough to make me one of the three finalists for the job. A second finalist was the longtime university provost and chief academic officer, a professor of fluid mechanics in the Engineering School. And the third was the Indian American chair of the Women's Studies Department at Clemson University.

Each of us had to make public talks to faculty, students, staff, and alumni, who could listen to us and then express their views to the search committee. The student daily newspaper urged the appointment of the women's studies candidate while the Faculty Senate supported the university provost. Alumni voices were relatively muted, though the Twelfth Man Club, an organization dedicated to supporting the football team, argued that no one should be appointed who did not have a proven record of supporting football.

The board of trustees probably chose me because I had a record of effective fundraising and balancing budgets. Also, I was the least controversial of the three candidates, though none of the board members ever said that to me in so many words. In my public talk, I stressed I wanted to help strengthen every academic department at the university and would raise funds to do so. That mollified most faculty. I also stressed that I was committed to enhancing the numbers of Black and Hispanic faculty and students. And I was a fan of athletics. One line that everyone cheered was, "I'm tired of Nebraska State being in the shadow of the University of Nebraska. We have the talent, the energy, and the ambition in our faculty, students, staff, and alumni to take our place as one of the leading public universities in the country. If I'm chosen as president, and with your help, I'll make that happen."

The board was wary of the provost because he had presided over the academic life of the campus for a decade during which the university's overall academic standing had slipped, though it was still stronger than the University of Nebraska. And the board thought the Women's Studies Department chair had too little administrative experience.

One experience I had with the board of trustees seemed to strengthen my relationship with its members, though at the time I feared it would do just the reverse. While I was still Business School dean, one of the trustees at the time, a Business School alumna, came to me with a proposal to endow a chair in accounting, which had been her undergraduate major. She was extremely wealthy, thanks to her father's money, and was a major contributor to the governor, which was one reason for her appointment. She was short and almost painfully thin, with a face lift that looked like an open-and-shut case for medical malpractice. But she was used to getting her way and wanted everyone to know it. "I understand I cannot choose the chair holder," she told me, "but I insist on the right to veto any potential candidate. I'm worried that the faculty will choose some Marxist for the position."

"The faculty has full authority to choose its members," I told her. "I can tell them of your concern, but I cannot turn down the faculty's recommendation solely because of your opposition." She told the whole board of my refusal of her "simple request," and for a time I was worried about the outcome. But all the other board members supported my position. As one of them told me privately, it showed I have "both backbone and balls."

Why did I want the job? Most of all because I loved the university. It was almost impossible for me to walk down a street in Nebraska, particularly in the northwestern part of the state, without people coming up to me to introduce themselves and say they were graduates of the university—or that one of their children, nieces, nephews, or other relatives went to the university.

In addition, unlike the four campuses of the University of Nebraska, the main campus of Nebraska State is truly beautiful. Situated in the Sand Hills of the northwestern part of the state, all the buildings are made of sandstone and have a coherence and cohesion lacking in most public universities. This was because most of the buildings were constructed at almost the same time from 1822 through 1825. The state legislature had decided a new public university was needed and the state's wealthiest hog farmer, Clarence

Rossiter—he was also among the richest men in the country—offered to pay for all twenty-four initial buildings if they were built around a giant courtyard that bore his name. A large and lovely fountain is in the middle of Rossiter Quadrangle, modeled after the Trevi Fountain in Rome. I've always been grateful that Rossiter did not ask the Nebraska legislature to name the university after him, like the Ball brothers in Muncie, Indiana, for whom Ball State University is named.

The sandstone walls of the Rossiter Quadrangle buildings are a foot thick, which keeps the buildings cool in the summer and warm in the winter. Shallow arches are at the front of each building, holding roofs that cover broad walkways. Rossiter Quadrangle is still the center of the university. Since it was built, scores of new academic and administrative buildings have been added, all built with sandstone. The roofs are also a uniform black tile, which adds to the cohesion of the campus. Beautiful islands of green—trees and plants—are scattered everywhere among the buildings. Simple fountains that throw up water and let it drop down into shallow pools add a sense of serenity.

And the Sand Hills region of Nebraska contains some of the most beautiful scenery in the state. A passage in "My Ántonia," one of my favorite novels by Willa Cather, Nebraska's leading writer, captured that beauty: "As I looked about me I felt that the grass was the country, as the water is the sea. The red of the grass made all the great prairie the colour of wine-stains, or of certain seaweeds when they are first washed up. And there was so much motion in it; the whole country seemed, somehow, to be running."

But the attraction of the presidency was much more than the beauty of the campus and its surroundings. I saw a chance to enhance the university in preparing our students for their careers and for their social and civic lives as well. I also saw an opportunity to help the economic development of the region, which was among the poorest and least developed areas of the state. Particularly important, I saw a chance to do things together with Emma in ways that we had not been able to do before. A public university presidency was definitely a two-person job if the president was fortunate enough to have a partner who enjoyed joint public activities.

Emma had already been an active board member of the county's United Way and soon was chosen as chair. This involved active fund-raising. She came to know the leaders of the business community throughout the Sand Hills region and a lot about the lives of those who worked in the Raytheon factory, which was the largest employer in town, apart from the university. And it was key that Emma was enthusiastic about the job and the prospect of our collaborating in the myriad of public events that presidents need to attend. I can still hear her say, "Let's do it!" when I told her I had been offered the job. In the years since then, she has occasionally grumbled, "Why in the world did we take on these headaches and heartaches." But most of the time, she was full of gratitude for our good fortune, just as I was.

My biggest regret from the moment I became president, and perhaps even before, was that I shortchanged the twins in terms of the time and attention they deserved from me. I became a workaholic as dean, and that weakness became even more acute during my first year as president. Launching both an academic agenda and a financial campaign to fund it was endlessly time-consuming, along with all the other issues that landed on my desk. Emma became increasingly frustrated that I was not available at home to assist the girls with their homework or help them learn to drive. Dinners had been an almost sacred family happening—a time when the girls, Emma, and I could share the events of the day. And I was late or absent for too many dinners as well.

Two incidents in that first year shamed me. First, I missed Emma's birthday. We had a tradition of celebrating by going to a hamburger joint near the campus. The morning of her birthday, a crisis exploded on the campus when a hangman's noose was spray-painted on the door of the Black Culture Center. I could have let the dean of students and the campus police handle it but instead spent the day crafting a statement to the university community and then, in the evening, leading an open meeting for students to talk about the explosive situation. I didn't even think to call Emma.

The second incident was when I missed music night at the girls' school. The girls had practiced for weeks, preparing to play a Bach duet in A minor for violin and cello. This time I was meeting with a group of faculty upset about a cost-cutting measure in the university's benefits program. Even though the state of Nebraska handles benefits for all public employees, including those at the university, the faculty thought that if I really cared about the matter, I could do something. The meeting stretched on into the evening, with lots of yelling by outraged faculty, and I forgot the concert.

More generally, looking back, I realize that I too often let my ambition shove aside what I should have been doing for my girls. Just at the time when adolescent girls need time with both parents, I was shortchanging them. This was particularly true since they were sixteen when I started as president, and they could drive to school. Up to that point, I had driven them every morning and at least then had a chance to catch up.

Except for missing family dinners, I did have time with Emma, even more time than when I was at the bank, because we did so much as a team and grew closer as a result. Put an emphasis on the word "public" in thinking about the roles of a public university president and a partner because we quickly found there are no secrets on a campus.

It was hot on August 1, 2015, the day before we moved to the president's house, and we went shopping for groceries. We were both in shorts and T-shirts. We walked into Kroger as we had so often in the past, but as we walked up and down the aisles, we noticed something different. Other shoppers were staring at us. Even friends whom we had known for years seemed suddenly to stop talking when they saw us coming. And they edged away from getting too near us. I whispered to Emma that I felt my fly must be open. Emma laughed and said she wondered if she had lipstick on her teeth. It may seem naive, but we couldn't figure out what was going on.

It was not until we were walking home that someone we did not know waved and said, "Hello, Mr. President. Quite a contrast to your predecessor." I knew what he meant, because my predecessor, Enzo Enrico, always wore three-button suits, a vest, and a watch chain with his Phi Beta Kappa key. Once you got to know him, he was a nice guy but very formal. The only useful advice Enrico ever gave me was,

"Don't worry about the dress code at Nebraska State—whatever you are wearing is the dress code."

We suddenly knew what had happened. We hadn't changed. Our roles in relation to those around us had changed. We were the president and first lady of Nebraska State. Those other shoppers had never seen a president who wasn't dressed as though he were going to a funeral. They had never seen a president other than Enrico.

As well as going to scores of alumni events, Emma and I went together to the Nebraska State Fair, for example, where the university had a large tent. Our School of Agriculture put on a show about what it was doing for Nebraska, with separate pens for cattle, horses, mules, chickens, and more. When one of our students won the blue ribbon for raising the biggest pig at the fair, I posed for a picture with her until the pig crapped all over my shoes.

One of the many changes we made was to insist that no more alumni activities in Nebraska and beyond could be held at country clubs and other facilities that discriminated—not just against Jews but against anyone based on race, gender, ethnicity, religion, or sexual orientation. This immediately eliminated lots of places where our alumni used to meet—particularly single-sex eating clubs and country clubs that did not allow persons of color to join. Yet somewhat to our surprise, we have never heard a single antisemitic remark during our entire time at the university. Occasionally, some alumnus would volunteer, "Some of my best friends are Jews," which may have been code for antisemitism. I am sure they would never say, "Some of my best friends are Christian." But I learned to let those remarks pass. I did hear a handful of comments about "those people" when directed at the small numbers of Black and Hispanic people living in Catherville. The much more serious challenge was enhancing the numbers of Black and Hispanic faculty, staff, and students.

It was also important to make gay students, faculty, and staff feel welcomed at the university, and this was a big shift from my predecessor. Perhaps because Enrico was a strict Catholic, or perhaps because he really thought homosexuality was a sin, he resisted having university recognition for gay, transgender, and bisexual programs and events on campus. This did not stop them from happening, but I got an earful when I became president about what a negative effect the silent antigay atmosphere had on everyone in the university community and on student admissions, as well as faculty and staff hiring. Enrico also blocked installation of condom machines in the student residences. This triggered a front-page blast in the student newspaper, but Enrico refused to back down. And I was told that the Theater Department had wanted to perform *Angels in America* and *The Vagina Monologues* but was quietly pressed by the president's office to choose other plays.

5

On July 1, 2015, I officially became president of Nebraska State University. I spent most of the next three months listening to faculty, staff, students, alumni, and legislators talk about their hopes and their concerns for the university. Emma joined me at most of those gatherings except when her teaching or our girls required her. And we both gained an increasing sense of what a joy it was to be doing so much together.

I tried to keep reminding myself that I could respectfully disagree with someone's position, but should try never to make it personal. And I needed to be especially careful never to lose my temper. Both the faculty and the alumni included some irritating individuals who liked nothing better than bad-mouthing something I did or didn't do. After a few battles with members of this group, I came to realize that squabbling with them did little but lower my self-esteem and whatever esteem most others had for me.

Over the next three years, Emma and I visited each of the ninety-three counties in Nebraska, usually for what were billed as "coffee and conversation" sessions sponsored by the county Chambers of Commerce or Rotary Clubs and were open to everyone. Nebraska State owned a small signal plane. It held four passengers and we used it whenever flying was faster than driving. I also had a wonderful driver, named Dave, who enabled me to work while he was driving. Emma and I soon felt like hyperactive politicians running for office. But this was a chance to learn about the people of Nebraska, their hopes and worries and, most important, their sense of what the university was doing and what it could do better.

I quickly realized that most of those with whom I met had little sense of the university's role in supporting the state and especially its economy. Our Office of Public Affairs was cranking out press releases extolling various happenings at the university, but no one paid attention to those releases.

I soon decided the university needed a new director of that office. As a result, my first personnel decision was to tell that director it was time for him to take early retirement, or I would fire him. Within a week, I hired Wanda Season, the deputy editor of the *Omaha World Herald*, whom I knew from my days as a banker. I also knew she had been frustrated in her position because she was unable to move as fast as she thought necessary to expand the digital editions of the newspaper and to strengthen its reach via social media. Both tasks were also essential for the university to reach the citizens of Nebraska, and Season was excited by the challenge of building the means to do so from the ground up.

Enrico had issued an annual report, "The State of the University," which he read at a session in the main campus auditorium and was shown via Zoom to the two regional campuses. Few faculty or staff and even fewer students bothered to show up or watch it. I decided to rearrange the heading of Enrico's report and title my inaugural speech "Our University in the State," focusing on what the state had a right to expect from the university and what the university had an obligation to provide to the state. The speech was covered in local newspapers throughout the state. In each county Emma and I visited, we made a point of talking with the editors of the local newspapers, and Season followed up by sending them copies of the speech and a personal note from me. Many, though not all, the newspapers carried at least excerpts from the speech, along with a story, and some carried the whole talk.

One sentence in the speech was sharply criticized by evangelical clergy from their pulpits throughout Nebraska: "This university must commit itself to welcoming women and men of every race, religion, and ethnic background, and also to the entire lesbian, gay, bisexual, transgender, and queer community." (I thought it important to spell out the terms rather than just say "LGBTQ community," in part for emphasis and in part because I suspected many in the audience would not know what the initials meant.) I thought there might be some backlash, but I had no idea how fierce the backlash would be. The fact that the sentence was singled out for praise in the student newspaper, *The Sentinel*, only added fuel to the criticism.

I knew I would have to reach out to clergy of all faiths, with special attention to evangelicals, to minimize what could easily become efforts to undermine my agenda. This led me to invite to a breakfast meeting all the clergy in the area surrounding the Catherville campus. A few refused because of my LGBTQ reference, but I received acceptances from twenty-nine of the thirty-four clergy whom I invited. "Small-group experiences are key," I said to them, "to whether students at this campus thrive or fall through the cracks. Experiences with faith-based groups are particularly important to ensuring that they thrive." Together we worked out a series of informal arrangements that made it easy for the clergy to be in touch with students who might be interested in joining their places of worship.

I also realized that many of our students came from towns smaller than their campus dorms and thought religious diversity meant two synods of the Lutheran church. So I encouraged the clergy to reach out to students who were not of their faiths to explain those faiths in simple terms, so students would come to respect all religions as important parts of the lives of their fellow students.

For example, I said to the head of the Newman Center, "Catholics represent about a quarter of Americans who go to church, but I suspect most students who are not Catholic are bewildered by some Catholic doctrines and beliefs." I told the clergy that we would publish a "Welcome to Your Faith" booklet that all freshmen would receive in their orientation packet. The booklet included key points that clergy of each faith wanted to emphasize. We also held evening sessions in freshmen residences when two students from a particular religion would explain what their faith meant to them. One of those sessions always included two students who explained why they were atheists.

The only person I invited to the meeting who did not even respond to my invitation was the rabbi at Hillel. In fact, as I learned, he was almost never on the campus except for the High Holidays. After the meeting, I called the head of Hillel in Washington, DC. "I'm the first Jewish president of Nebraska State University," I said, "and I can't find the Hillel rabbi. He is apparently almost never on campus. This is a real problem for me."

"I'll come out there next week with my assistant," he responded, "and if what you tell me seems accurate, I'll fire the rabbi, and we will find a new one."

He was as good as his word, and after three days talking to faculty, staff, and students, the Hillel national director came to me and said, "I just fired the rabbi for failure to perform his duties. Please help me find a new one. And please also help in building a new Hillel, for the current Hillel building is a mess." In the next few months, an energetic young woman was hired as the new Hillel rabbi. She had just graduated from Hebrew Union College in Cincinnati. And Emma had headed a successful campaign to raise the funds needed for a new Hillel building.

I asked a Catholic nun to give the invocation and a Presbyterian minister to give the benediction at the end of my inauguration ceremony. She had spent her career at the Newman Center on the campus and was beloved by all who knew her. When I asked her to speak, I said, "I ask you to be mindful of two matters. First, Nebraska State is a public university, so please do not mention Jesus Christ. And second, please keep your remarks to two minutes or less because we want to keep the whole ceremony under an hour." Sister Teresa readily agreed. But when she got up to speak, she threw her arms out and talked and talked and talked. It was close to ten minutes before she sat down.

"Sister," I said to her afterward, "what you said was meaningful to everyone, but you promised me you would talk for less than two minutes."

In reply, she laughed and said, "Mr. President, for thirty years I have longed to preach and have been unable to do so, while every priest gets to preach, whatever his abilities. I was not going to let this opportunity pass in just two minutes." I laughed and said I understood.

One of the challenges I faced as president, which came in my first week in office, happened when the Catherville newspaper ran a story celebrating that Nebraska State was the home of the first Black fraternity in the country, Kappa Psi Alpha, founded at the height of Jim Crow bigotry in the country. Until the 1960s, racial segregation was required in campus residences, as was true at public universities across the country, and the fraternity was a legacy of that time. The dean of students, Alexia Fisher, met with me and reminded me that the university has a policy precluding racial, religious, or gender discrimination "in any form on or at any university facility." I certainly knew about the policy since I had expanded its scope to include sexual orientation, as I had promised in my inaugural address.

"I feel I have an obligation to enforce the policy," Fisher said, "and that means ordering the fraternity to admit non-Black students in order to stay recognized by the university."

I thought for a few minutes and then responded, "This fraternity is one of the few places on campus, perhaps the only place other than the football and basketball locker rooms, where Black students can be with a substantial number of other Black students. Please do not worry about the issue. I will take care of it." And I did nothing further.

My family was delighted to move into the president's house, a beautiful 10,000-square-foot center-entrance, three-story Georgian sandstone home built by Clarence Rossiter in the middle of the campus. The grounds surrounding the house were stunning, filled with numerous flower beds and a small reflecting pool. Before we moved, we managed to brighten the house and make it feel like our home. The wife of one of our good friends in the History Department was an interior decorator, and she helped us renovate the first floor. We took off the heavy drapes on all the first-floor rooms and filled them with our own furniture, along with lots of pictures of our family. Emma's art adorned the walls, along with paintings by some of her friends with whom she exchanged pieces. We used the first floor for parties, university gatherings, and dinners with friends and family members from around the country.

The second floor included our bedroom, with a study and TV room attached, and two smaller bedrooms for the girls. The third floor had three spacious bedrooms where major donors to the university and other distinguished guests could stay. It was a special joy for us to have leading artists and musicians in our home. We had an especially good chance to come to know these women and men as more than just leaders in their fields when they were our house guests. When Menachem Pressler and the Beaux Arts Trio stayed with us, for example, we had a lovely dinner together followed by their performance of Beethoven's Triple Concerto in our living room. Then they asked Abby and Amy to play while they held a brief master class for the girls.

Our only problem with guests came when a trio of young musicians were staying on the third floor while they gave a series of concerts and master classes at the School of Music. We had a house manager who made all the arrangements for university guests when they stayed with us. On the day after they arrived, the manager came to me and told me, "The third floor reeks of pot. It really stinks. What should I do?"

I was waiting for the musicians when they returned from their concert. "You'll have to leave," I said firmly, "if you smoke pot in our house again. Further, I will tell the School of Music and the school newspaper the reason for canceling the rest of your concerts and master classes." The musicians apologized, and from then on during their stay, the air was clear on the third floor.

The president's house was our home, but it was also an entertainment center. We loved living there, and Emma, with some help, made it a comfortable place for us to live with our two teenage girls. It had a quiet elegance, without being too formal. But it was also a wonderful place to have a party, and we had lots of them. We regularly hosted gatherings of key state legislators, leading alumni, prominent faculty, those we were wooing to join the faculty, and outstanding students, as well, of course, as donors. Emma and I tried to alternate large gatherings—we could host receptions for two hundred or more and dinners for up to fifty—with small parties of twelve or less. And these included parties of just our friends, which we paid for, as well as university functions. Fortunately we had lots of help to cook and serve at the gatherings, though Emma was a great cook and often took charge of the kitchen when we were just entertaining friends.

The campus is large, almost 1,200 acres, and the president's house was located on the highest ground within the academic campus center. Students coming to or from their campus residences to the classrooms and labs generally walked through the lawn and beautiful garden in front the president's house. Our golden retriever, Becky, had been with us since our girls were infants, and Becky liked to lie on that lawn so she could be petted by all the students coming by. They missed their own dogs at home and were comforted by Becky. If robbers ever had come to the house, Becky would have shown them where we kept the silver. But in all other respects, she was an ideal companion for our family.

We sold our own house, located near the edge of the campus, feeling that when my time as president ended, we would likely not stay in the Catherville area. Enrico and his wife had moved to a house a mile or so from the campus, and while he never offered advice unless I asked for it, I always thought it unwise for a former president to stick around.

There's an old story I like about an unnamed university president who, as he was leaving his position, gave three envelopes to the incoming president. "Whenever you are in serious trouble," the outgoing president said, "open one of these envelopes." In her first year, the new president got into trouble with some faculty members and opened the first envelope. "Blame it on your predecessor," it said. And she did. In her second year, she had a hard time with some students and opened the second envelope. "Blame it on your predecessor," it said. And she did. During her third year, the president had a dispute with an alumni group and opened the third envelope. "Prepare three envelopes," it said. And she did.

Emma had a busy schedule teaching in the Fine Arts Department, but we still had lots of time together at various university events. We also made a pact that we would have at least one night a week to ourselves and Amy and Abby. They were sixteen when we moved into the president's home and loved each having a bedroom of their own. And they were overjoyed that the house had an elevator, installed by a former president for his elderly mother who lived with him. Amy and Abby delighted in riding up and down on the elevator until Emma and I limited them to three rides a day.

In my first months as president, I came to realize how little was known about Nebraska State outside of the Sand Hills region. We were in the shadow of the University of Nebraska, and as a result, the light of publicity about our academic strengths and economic benefits to Nebraska rarely reached across the state.

My response to this concern was to launch four efforts to enhance the university's visibility in Nebraska and beyond, and over time they seemed to work. The first was to make the research work going on in the School of Agriculture much better known throughout the state. I took advantage of the fact that the university owned both a public radio station and a public television station—KNSU. It was part of Nebraska Public Media, a network of nine other public radio and television stations in the state. Many of our popular programs were carried throughout Nebraska and beyond.

We started a monthly radio talk show that was hosted by one of the ablest faculty members of the School of Agriculture. She put together a show called *Farming Nebraska Today and Tomorrow*, which featured university faculty and graduate students from the School of Agriculture talking about the practical benefits of their research for Nebraska farmers. One episode, I recall, was a live showing of the best way to assist cows to give birth to their calves when help was needed.

In addition, farmers could call into the show and have their questions answered by one of a team of graduate students, each an expert in a particular field. When a graduate student did not know the answer to a question, a follow-up with the answer was always promised to the inquiring farmer, and those answers were also repeated on the air. The result was the most popular radio show in Nebraska focused on its most important business, farming. The state had over 45,000 farms, and the show was heard by a significant share of those who worked on those farms. It was difficult to grow crops in the Sand Hills soil, and this was why hogs and cattle were the major agricultural products. But this also meant that farmers who grew corn, wheat, soybeans, and other products were eager for sound advice based in science. The show was such a success that another was started with a focus on cooking.

Second, we launched a one-hour TV show that I moderated once a week for twelve weeks a year. We called it *Pro & Con* and invited two different university faculty members for each episode to join me in discussing controversial issues, though we stayed away from hot-button political topics. Nebraska was a deeply red state, and it was too dangerous for the university to address an issue like abortion. One faculty member, with expertise in the relevant field, argued each side of such questions as whether the morality of an artist should be included in considering the merits of the artist's work. Should the fact that Picasso lived with many different women affect our judgments about his art? Is creativity more a matter of genetics or of a nurturing environment? These and similar questions made for lively debates that displayed the talents of our leading faculty members. The show was picked up by other public-broadcasting stations, and I often received letters about it from as far away as California and New York.

The third project was a monthly column that I wrote for the Gannett newspaper chain. This happened because the publisher of the paper was a Nebraska State graduate whom I contacted for advice about how to make the campus visible outside the state. He suggested my column with the understanding that individual Gannett newspapers could print or not any particular column. This meant that over one hundred daily papers and over one thousand weekly papers received and considered each column. The publisher was sure that many would print most of them. And they did. I wrote on a wide range of issues, some relating to higher education but many involving other topics that interested me.

Like my TV show, I stayed away from controversial issues, since many readers assumed I was writing for the university. But every once in a while, I got in hot water over a column, like one I did about criminal punishments in which I said I would rather have my hand cut off than spend a year in a maximum-security prison. Some readers assumed I was arguing for cutting off hands as punishment, which was not my intent, as I explained in a subsequent column.

Finally, another graduate of Nebraska State bought the rights to the *Saturday Evening Post,* once among the most widely read magazines in the country. I suggested to him that I write occasional "Bible Stories" that related teachings from stories in the Hebrew Bible to current times—such as the stories about Job, Jonah and the whale, and Abraham and Isaac. Evangelical Christians were 25 percent of Nebraska's population at the time, and these stories became extremely popular among that group. The fact that I was a Jew seemed to add to its interest around the state.

I also used a new advertising firm to prepare the two-minute TV spots that Nebraska State could show on national television during our basketball and football games. In the past, those spots had looked as though they could be about any major public university in the country—pictures of buildings and students peering into microscopes. I decided to do something different. The firm we chose was known for its appeal to youth.

One of the best spots it created was my interview with a star basketball player. I asked him what his most unnerving moment as a Nebraska State freshman was, thinking he would refer to some time when he was yelled at by his coach. Instead, he answered, "When I had to give a five-minute talk in our required public-speaking class. Because I learned as a freshman to be a confident speaker, I now feel confident about much more as well." Seeing this young man, used to playing before thousands of fans in our arena and many more via television, confessing to being nervous in giving his first speech made a big and positive impact on everyone who saw it.

The ad created by the firm that I liked best showed a young man in shadows, his back to the camera. He was talking in a foreign language, which was actually Japanese. After a full minute, he swirled his chair around as the lights came up. To the surprise of every viewer, he was a young white man and not Asian. "Here at Nebraska State," he said in English, "you can become fluent in any one of fifty-seven languages.

Come join me at this great university." The ad was a hit and won a prize for the advertising firm.

Dealing with the university's external visibility turned out to be a much easier challenge to handle than grappling with its internal problems. The first hurdle was to completely change the budget system for the university. I knew most other colleges and universities followed a system similar to the Nebraska State one I was abandoning. I thought that system was ridiculous when I was a dean and vowed I would change it if I had a chance. As president, I had that chance.

Under the old system, schools and their deans essentially had financial responsibility only for the costs of compensating their faculty and staff. Almost all other costs of running the university were paid centrally by the university administration. As a result, schools had no incentive to save money by being certain, for example, that faculty did not have two offices—many, in fact, did—or to ensure that schools minimized costs, such as utilities.. Similarly, all tuition went to the university administration, so there was no incentive for schools to try to increase student enrollments in their courses. Schools did benefit from their own fundraising, but the university kept tight control over which potential donors could be asked for contributions.

I knew a few other universities had adopted what was called responsibility-centered management, and one of my first hires was Andrew Ku, the budget director at the University of Pennsylvania, which was among those institutions. Ku became our senior associate vice president for finance and administration. My charge to him was to oversee the steps needed for Nebraska State to become the first public university in the country to adopt responsibility-centered management.

Ku looked like an accountant straight out of Hollywood. He was always serious, with glasses that had such thick lenses it was hard to see his eyes. He even wore a green eyeshade when he was pouring over the details of budgets.

When the announcement was made that Ku would take charge of the shift to responsibility-centered management, an immediate outcry came from the weaker schools and the weaker faculty. The loudest screams came from the School of Arts and Sciences. The complaints focused on the fear that the School of Business would start its own courses in economics, statistics, and similar quantitative fields, syphoning students away from the existing courses in the School of Arts and Sciences. Similar concerns were raised about the School of Medicine starting its own courses in biology and other sciences. And the same worries arose about the School of Engineering launching courses in computer science—the most popular major at Nebraska State—which was located in the School of Arts and Sciences. It was not hard to work out a set of protocols that precluded such "mission creep" by the Schools of Business, Medicine, and Engineering, the three financially strongest schools. A score of other issues were raised, and over time, they were resolved.

One of the toughest was the concern of the School of Music, which was heavily subsidized on a per-student basis compared to other schools. It was also one of the best schools of music in the country. Ku and I made the case that the university would continue to subsidize some academic units more than others, but instead of the academic strengths being judged solely by the president in consultation with the provost, as had been true in the past, the judging would be made by a group of distinguished faculty and senior administrators, and those units that showed significant improvement would be rewarded, not just those that were already outstanding.

A score of other issues faced me in the first year, when everything I did was for the first time. Many of the issues involved money from the state legislature. When I visited the chair of the House Budget Committee to ask for an increase in state support for the university, he looked at me and smiled. "You are a nice fellow," he said, "but when I hear your plea from my constituents, I will start paying attention." That gave me the idea of launching a new organization of alumni that would lobby throughout the state on behalf of the university. We called it Huskies for Higher Education. The University of Nebraska teams are known as the Cornhuskers, of course, but we saw no reason that should preclude our adopting this name.

Using money donated to the university via our foundation, I and several trustees interviewed three grassroots organizing firms and chose one to design and build the new organization. We had alumni captains in every legislative district, along with as many alumni lieutenants as we could recruit. We kept them up-to-date on university needs while periodically sending them university caps, beer mugs, and other swag. And twice a year, we invited all the state legislators, along with the alumni captains and lieutenants, to a university football or basketball game, followed by sessions involving leading faculty talking about their research that directly benefited the state.

Despite these efforts, during a recession, the legislature reduced the higher-education budgets for all the public universities in the state, which made our already tight financial situation even more precarious. Fortunately, the shift to responsibility-centered management gave school deans and the heads of our two regional campuses—called chancellors—an incentive to increase their revenues and reduce their costs. I promised to try to look favorably on every entrepreneurial effort the campus leaders proposed. As a result, a host of imaginative proposals were made. There were two I particularly liked and endorsed with enthusiasm.

At the Catherville campus—the university's flagship, where I was the chancellor as well as university president—the vice president for development came to me with a simple question: What should be for sale?

"We have endowed faculty," he said, "and even one endowed school, the School of Music. All have the name of the endower—a person or commercial firm. We have endowed scholarships and endowed speaker series—again, all with the name of the endower. But what about a single course?" Could we have English 100 brought by the *Catherville Crescent*, the major local newspaper in town? In collaboration with the Faculty Senate, we put together an ad hoc committee of faculty to consider the issue. I did not ask them whether we could do this but rather how we could do this while remaining consistent with our university's standards of academic integrity. The ad hoc committee developed a set of simple guidelines that precluded situations in which there could be an obvious clash between the interests of the class sponsor and what was being taught in the class and proposed that any course that was being considered for naming needed to be reviewed by the committee. I agreed, and soon we had seven named courses, five by individuals and two by firms, one a law firm that sponsored a communications course and one a radio station that supported a music course.

Our two regional campuses were facing even tougher belt-tightening as a result of the state budget cuts, because those campuses were less well funded per student than the Catherville campus. This always seemed unfair to me, as it certainly did to the faculty, students, and staff on those campuses. But since it was a pattern that was replicated throughout the country, there was no chance I could do anything about it. In California, for example, the University of California was much better funded than the California State University campuses, and those campuses were better funded than the California community colleges.

That system was perverse because it was just the reverse of student need. The argument always made was that the flagship campuses were dedicated to research as well as teaching, but the argument was often belied by the facts. At the demand of one of our trustees, I commissioned a graduate student to count the numbers of publications by the faculty of the Catherville campus after they received tenure and found that the average was less than one publication—not per year but ever. When the school newspaper, *The Sentinel,* published that result, the Faculty Senate immediately prepared a counter report arguing that many of the publications were books that often take years or even a lifetime to complete. But the revelation was at least a catalyst for the Faculty Senate to revise the faculty handbook so that research productivity must be taken into account in setting faculty compensation on the Catherville campus.

That shift did not help the regional campuses, and the budget cuts had an even worse impact on them. Their chancellors, however, brainstormed with their senior staffs and came up with some imaginative ideas. This is the one I liked best. The two campuses were charging $24 per course unit, so an average full-time student taking four three-unit courses would pay about $100 per quarter. In addition, the average student was paying about $66 or so for health, parking, and other fees. The idea was for the two campuses to set up a boutique summer learning program for students from wealthy parents who, for one reason or another, needed remedial work to transfer to the Catherville campus. The program was limited to four hundred students per summer who, in classes of not more than twenty students, learned math and writing skills from the most accomplished teachers, who taught these courses on an overload basis. The program offered fifty sections per summer for a student fee of $5,000 and generated $2,000,000 per year. The fifty faculty members received half of that amount—$20,000 each—and each campus gained $500,000. The Faculty Senate at each campus had an impassioned debate about the proposal, some arguing that the plan was unfair to poor students, and the campus should not discriminate based on wealth. But when each campus chancellor promised to use their funds for student scholarships, the plan was adopted.

I came to the presidency fully realizing that academics at the university had steadily slipped over the past decade. I was determined to focus on making the best departments world-class and shoring up the others. At the main campus in Catherville, we had excellent Schools of Agriculture, Business, Engineering, Medicine, and Music. The School of Education and the School of Arts and Sciences had a number of first-rate departments. But those two schools were also reputed each to have a couple of weak departments. The School of Social Work was very weak, by reputation, and close to losing its accreditation for not making adequate clinical placements available to its students. I told myself I needed a way to find out whether reputations matched reality for every school and department.

Faculty at the Catherville campus were expected to teach an average of six courses spread over three quarters and spend a significant amount of time on research. In fact, as I learned, the actual average was closer to four courses per year. And some faculty taught only three courses. Most faculty managed to find a way to avoid teaching at least one course per year by doing committee work or some other activity. At the same time, most faculty at the regional campuses were teaching at least nine courses per year, and many were teaching more.

If I had simply announced those facts and said we needed a new faculty accountability system, I knew the Catherville Faculty Senate would be up in arms, claiming that I was encroaching on their academic prerogatives. Instead, I went quietly to one of the university trustees, Jared Carter, who was often vocal in finding fault with some feature of how we managed the university. Usually, he was a pain in my tail. But this time I thought I might use Carter to my advantage. I told him of the facts and asked him to demand publicly at the next trustee meeting that I commission a study of faculty workload, including teaching, and ask the trustees to pass a resolution to that end, one that would include a mandate to tie faculty compensation to "workload and performance."

"Please leave open the definition of 'workload and performance,'" I asked Carter. "But it's important to make clear that if the trustees are not satisfied with the way the issue is being handled, they will develop their own definition." I told Carter that I would respond to the resolution by saying, "It's important for the faculty to have responsibility for academic issues, including teaching, but the university will, of course, carry out the trustees' mandate." For once, Carter and I were in full agreement. He loved the idea of a conspiracy between us, he said, and promised not to tell anyone, including other trustees about what he instantly called "our plan."

And the plan went off just as I had hoped. It took two years of work by each school and department to obtain full audits that showed publicly what faculty members had been doing or not doing. And several times I had to lean hard on the Faculty Senate, saying that whatever problems it was having in developing a plan, the situation would be far worse if the trustees developed their own plan. In the end, the Faculty Senate, in collaboration with the provost, revealed the results of the audit. Schools and department chairs were called on to ensure that each faculty member develop a work plan once a year for the following year and that, at the end of each year, the chairs would monitor and report to the Faculty Senate the extent to which those work plans had been carried out. The language was a bit vague in places, but the very threat that the trustees might be involved gave a big boost, I am convinced, to the quality and quantity of teaching on the Catherville campus. I was much less sure that it made any difference in terms of research productivity but decided that would be too much of a hornet's nest to deal with, at least for a time.

Academic quality was even more uneven at the two regional campuses. Faculty there primarily focused on teaching. But more than half of the teaching was done by adjunct faculty who were paid by the course, and many of those faculty had to travel back and forth between the two regional campuses to make ends meet. I became convinced we needed to review teaching quality at both campuses as well as at the Catherville campus. I had made promoting student success a centerpiece of my inaugural address, and I needed to make good on that commitment.

The provost and I charged the university Faculty Senate with producing a plan, making clear that otherwise the trustees would develop their own plan. I was again working in confidential concert with Carter. After much discussion, the result was that every department on all three campuses was required to establish criteria for annually evaluating teaching quality and processes for applying the criteria. Some of the resulting criteria were a bit vague, but the issue of teaching quality had been addressed head on.

In my first year, with the help of an outside consultant, I organized an academic planning process that included the three campuses and all eight schools. A key part of the academic planning effort was to include our two regional campuses, each located about eighty miles from Catherville. They both had been started because of political pressures from local state legislators in the sprawling Sand Hills region. Those legislators understandably felt that young people in their areas deserved a college education even though they could not afford to travel to Catherville. Since there were no community colleges in the Sand Hills area, the problem was a real one. Faculty who taught at the regional campuses, students who learned there, and staff who worked there felt like second-class citizens, and with good reason. When one of the regional campuses needed a new car, for example, it had to buy the car, drive it to the Catherville campus to be registered, and then drive home. The course offerings and facilities were more modest than those at the main campus, and the faculty and staff salaries were lower.

One of my first steps as president was to coin the slogan "One university, three front doors." I stopped using the term "regional campus" in my public talks and instead gave the campuses the names of the two communities where they were located—St. Peter and Monterey. The university repair shop even made a small model of a triangular building with a door on each side and "One University" emblazoned on the top. The model has pride of place at all the trustee and other university-wide meetings.

We also set up a fund to support research projects that joined faculty and students at Catherville and the regional campuses. Emma organized a traveling art show displaying works of faculty and students from all three campuses.

Further, we established a policy that when there was a temporary opening for an instructor at the Catherville campus, faculty at the two other campuses were encouraged to apply. PhD students at the Catherville campus were encouraged to teach at those campuses. And undergraduate students from those campuses were allowed to transfer to the Catherville campus if they had a satisfactory grade point average.

One other important initiative was a new program to honor outstanding teachers on each campus. Every year two faculty members from each campus were chosen by student vote. They formed an organization known as the Teaching Excellence Academy (TEA). The TEA faculty received a $5,000 one-time bonus and a $2,000 permanent salary increase, in exchange for which they held workshops on good teaching on their own campuses.

Finally, and most important, with the trustees' approval I allocated one million dollars of the university's scarce reserves to support a new academic-planning process over five years. The Faculty Senate was hesitant at first about the move but endorsed it when its members learned that most of the funds were to be spent to pay faculty in each department on all three campuses to develop academic improvement plans and oversee their implementation. Over the first year, on each campus, every school—and every department within each school—was charged with developing a five-year plan to strengthen its teaching, research, and service to the state. Those plans had to include clear indicators of success over the five years. I chaired an ad hoc committee of deans and department chairs to review the plans and either approve them or send them back for more work.

After a year in office, the academic-planning process was going well, and I felt confident that it would help to strengthen academics throughout the campus. But athletics kept diverting me—especially football. And suddenly, athletics was not just a diversion; it was center stage because I had only six months to find an athletic director who would also serve as football coach. The countdown had begun.

The day after I met with the trustees, MacGruder was the first person I told about the trustees' charge to me—find a new athletic director / football coach, and do it in six months or get fired. We were in my office at 8:00 a.m., after I had sent him a message the night before saying I needed to see him urgently. He walked into my office dressed in a crumpled Nebraska State sweatshirt, looking like he had been up all night. I was almost sure he had come straight from working in his engineering lab. I quickly told him the news.

He looked at me in amazement and said, "Those bastards! Why didn't they just fire you on the spot instead of giving you an impossible task? Finding a new athletic director in just six months is bad enough. But insisting that he also be a winning football coach is absurd."

"I know," I replied, "but I'm going to try. And I need you to help me. You are the only person trusted by both the Athletic Department staff and the faculty. I want you to become interim athletic director for the next six months and to chair the search committee for a superstar to replace Knowland. You can say no, of course, and I will understand. You will still be my friend as well as my colleague. But I can't let those bastards, as you rightly called them, beat me without a fight. And with your help, I can—just maybe—win that fight. If I don't, at least I will know I tried as hard as I could."

I knew that MacGruder, as chair of the Faculty Athletics Committee, was respected by the entire Athletic Department. He was an engineering professor, one who had a long career in business before joining the Engineering School to head its joint-degree program with the Business School. We became good friends before either of us started at Nebraska State because my bank helped finance one of MacGruder's start-ups, a company called Fail-Safe that provided internet security for businesses.

MacGruder was almost hypnotically ugly with a scar running across the whole side of his face, from a childhood accident when he got too close to a model airplane's whirling propeller. Also, he had played rugby, which certainly contributed to his misshapen looks. But you forgot those looks soon after you start talking with him because he had an incandescent smile. He had a way of making anyone he talked with feel that she or he was the most important person with whom he could possibly have a conversation. In addition, he was a boisterous sports fan, and since he came to Nebraska State, had gone regularly to games and matches in almost every sport, women's and men's. He was also a totally sensible guy with a no-nonsense approach to solving problems quickly and, in the process, made those with whom he was working feel good.

To my great relief, MacGruder didn't hesitate. "I think you're nuts," he said, "but I don't want you to be nuts by yourself, so I'll help you in any way I can."

"You just won a place in my personal list of those marked to go to heaven. I can't thank you enough." And I gave him a big hug. "You'll not only get my gratitude; you'll receive a salary increase of twenty thousand dollars for the year and a half-year leave with pay at the end of the next six months, whatever the outcome of the search. You will have my full support, in making whatever changes, however radical, you think make sense."

"Just to be clear," he said emphatically, "I am out of this role at the end of six months. Now, what's the first step?"

"A public announcement is needed immediately—today. Everything has to happen quickly. I'll ask Season to come in and help us figure out whether I should tell the whole story of what I need to do to keep my job." I called Season, and she was with us within five minutes. Season was a twenty-eight-year-old Asian American woman whose parents came from Korea just before she was born. She could not be more than five feet tall and was thin as a flagpole. But she was whip-smart and had a tongue that was razor-sharp. "Oh, shit!" she exploded when I told her just what I had told MacGruder. "The trustees put you on a suicide course."

"Not suicide," I responded. "If I fail, it will not be because I didn't try."

Before she could say anything further, I asked her whether I should tell the university community and the public the whole story of the charge the trustees gave me and the consequences if I failed.

"That's just what you have to do," she quickly answered. "The story will leak out soon anyway. Bad news always does. If we issue a press release immediately and then have a press conference, we'll put the best spin we can on the story."

In the next hour, Season first called the local news media for a press conference at noon that day. Then she thought silently for about ten minutes and quickly wrote these words: "President Rosen announced today that a search will immediately be launched for a new athletic director who will also be football coach. The university trustees pressed President Rosen to quickly act and gave him a six-month deadline to find the right combination of talents to successfully lead the Athletic Department and the football program."

I read it and agreed. (I have hated split infinitives since my high school English teacher made students rewrite their papers if he found one. But it was too important to release the statement fast to quibble about grammar.) I did tell Season to add a few quotes from me: "Coach Knowland had amazing success as our football coach and our athletic director. He was a champion to the entire Nebraska State community and can never be replaced. But I am committed to finding the right leader who will stand on his shoulders and continue the great traditions of Nebraska State athletics and our remarkable successes on the football field."

I explained, "I know that's bullshit, but there's no need to rile up the Knowland fans even more."

While Season went off to release the statement and get ready for the press conference, I huddled further with MacGruder and worked out an intense schedule of meetings and steps over the next six months. Everything would have to work perfectly from the start to finish a search in that time. And in university administration, I knew that nothing ever works perfectly. But I was committed to try. I felt strangely liberated, knowing that I could do whatever I wanted to strengthen the university in the next six months because nothing would make any difference to the trustees unless we found and hired the right superstar. If we didn't, I would be toast. If we did, I would be a hero.

The press conference started off better than I expected. The reporters must have realized that the trustees had given me an impossible job and did not press me on whether I was angry at them.

"They have given me an assignment," I said, "and I'll do my best to fulfill that assignment."

"And do you expect to get fired if you fail?" I was asked.

"I don't expect to fail," I replied. "But yes, this is a test of whether the trustees feel they have confidence in my leadership of the university. And if I fail that test, I expect the trustees will look for another president."

Nebraska State obviously needed an interim football coach. MacGruder and I agreed it had to be Sonny Tizzo, who had been with Knowland from almost the start of his coaching career at Nebraska State University. Tizzo was a little guy with a face like a weasel, bulging eyes, and a body that looked like it had been drained of all its blood, leaving only skin and bones. He was an assistant coach under Knowland, and when Knowland became Athletic Director, Tizzo added Associate Athletic Director to his title.

We knew Tizzo was little more than Knowland's toady and that he lacked the necessary abilities to lead or even control the ego-intensive coaches. We felt we had little choice, however, but to appoint Tizzo as interim football coach since it was the middle of the season, and there was no other even plausible candidate.

At 1:00 p.m. that afternoon, I called Tizzo with the news. No surprise, he was delighted, particularly when I increased his salary, though not to Knowland's level. But I insisted that Tizzo resign as Associate Athletic Director, and he readily agreed. Under his leadership, the team lost three of its last four games, but most fans chalked this up to the trauma of Knowland's death.

Then I told Polly Porter to set up meetings starting at 2:00 p.m. that afternoon for MacGruder and me, each forty-five minutes apart: first, we would meet with nine assistant football coaches and seventeen football trainers and other football staff, and second, with all the coaches and staffs of the other teams. I also told her to schedule that night separate meetings with two groups of students—first, the football players; second, the captains of the other teams. We knew that not everyone could come, especially on such short notice. But I felt these steps needed to be taken and all in the same day.

The session with Tizzo, the assistant football coaches, and other football staff was short and unsurprising. All of them were supportive of Knowland and stressed how important it was to find a new coach in his image. They knew that new head football coaches brought with them assistant coaches from their former campuses, so they had to be nervous about their own jobs. But they didn't raise that issue, probably since they knew I could do nothing about it. They did tell us to be prepared to hear negative comments from other coaches and staff and to realize that those were just "sour grapes," triggered by the successes of the football team and the failures of many of the other teams. MacGruder and I left the meeting feeling we had done what we wanted to do—minimize the criticisms about me and my administration, criticisms that might make my job even tougher.

In our meeting with the coaches, I began by asking for their frank judgments about the state of the Athletic Department. I promised that the meeting was closed and that their comments would be kept in confidence. I also stressed that I needed their honest opinions. I knew that there was no way for me to keep coaches from telling reporters and others what had been said, but I thought they would speak more freely if I said that. In all events, I heard a flood of concerns over the next forty-five minutes.

Coach after coach, men as well as women, stood up and said that Knowland had run the department like a dictator, supporting his friends, who were mainly assistant football coaches, and denying support for the rest of the coaches and their teams. "It was his way or the highway." "He didn't talk; he just barked." Example after example poured out. The coach of the men's tennis team said Knowland had told him that tennis was a game for sissies and cut its funding and athletic scholarships. The coach of the women's soccer team said Knowland had looked at her one day and said her breasts looked like soccer balls. When she threatened to report him for sexual harassment, he countered that he would stop giving her any pay increases, despite the strong records of her teams. So she did nothing.

MacGruder and I came away realizing that much had to be done in the next six months. If our search was successful in that time, we didn't want the Athletic Department in disarray when the new director arrived. If our search was a failure, at least I wanted to be sure I was not leaving the department in a mess.

The meeting that night with over one hundred football players was both interesting and a bit surprising. I had expected uniform adulation for Knowland. Most of the starting players were enthusiastic. Some said he had been a surrogate father for them. But other players, many of whom spent most of their time during games on the bench, claimed that Knowland never made them feel part of the team. A few said he frequently made racist comments, and others nodded silently in agreement. "You're a Black boy and ought to be tougher than that," was a typical Knowland remark. We left that meeting commenting to each other that the new coach would have a lot of work to do.

MacGruder and I then met with the student captains of all the varsity teams to learn their views. The most troublesome issue I heard about was racism. Nebraska has only about 80,000 Black and 167,000 Hispanic people in a state of two million. The university had struggled to diversify its faculty and staff and to recruit Black and Hispanic students. Apart from the football and basketball teams, the campus had had little success before I became president.

The Black and Hispanic players complained loudly and with real anguish that there was no place on campus, other than the teams' locker rooms, where they felt they really belonged, apart from the one historically Black fraternity. They said that they were subject to frequent racial slurs by other students, including their teammates, and that there was no effort to enforce the campus policies against those misdeeds. They even told of finding the N-word painted on the lockers of all the Black players. Knowland, they said, refused to deal with the matter.

If my presidency survived this search, I silently said to myself, I must raise the funds needed to build a multicultural facility, with ample spaces for both a Black Culture Center and a Hispanic Culture Center. Those centers needed to be fundraising priorities among new campus facilities.

At the end of day 1 of my 182-day race to hire a new athletic director / football coach, I felt MacGruder and I had done all we could to ease tensions and contain potential problems within the athletic community. Now we had to get the search underway—fast. But before going to sleep that night, I called Franklin Adams and told him I wanted to report regularly to him what we were doing to find a new athletic director / football coach. I needed his help and advice, though I knew I could not completely count on him.

"I know we put you in a really tough spot," said Adams before I could speak. "But I hope you realize that the alternative was to fire you on the spot. As you must have guessed, three trustees were leaning that way, and I could tell a fourth was being increasingly persuaded to follow their lead. My only option was to propose the six-month plan. The rest of the trustees agreed, four of them reluctantly."

"I understand," I said, "though I wish it were otherwise. But now I want to propose that I talk to you at least once a week, so you know exactly what is going on in terms of the search. I may need your advice from time to time, and whatever happens, my calls will give you a record of what was done and why in case the search fails."

"We both hope that won't happen," he responded. "And certainly keep me apprised each week about what is going on."

I had hoped to limit the size of the search committee to six or eight members, but on reflection, that seemed impossible because key constituencies had to be represented. University rules required "representation from each relevant constituency." The requirement was added to the university handbook after a dictatorial president in the 1950s stacked every search committee with his toadies. The Faculty Senate threatened to censure him unless he agreed to the new rule, and it has been sacred text ever since.

Five constituencies had to be represented: coaches, Athletic Department staff, players and other students, faculty, and alumni. In addition, I wanted to include two athletic directors from other universities, ideally at least one of whom was or had also been a football coach. Too often search committees have no members who have any firsthand knowledge of the job in question. It's the blind leading the blind. Further, I thought we needed two representatives from each constituency to avoid the danger that a single representative might have too much influence—I've experienced that problem too often. This meant that our search committee would include twelve persons plus MacGruder as chair. I just hoped that number would not prove unlucky.

To identify the best committee members, MacGruder and I decided we would hold a series of small sessions during the next week and invite a group of leaders in each category—apart from the two other athletic directors—for informal discussions of athletics at Nebraska State. I thought this could lead to ten sensible people who would join with the two outside athletic directors and MacGruder to compose the search committee. I hoped the committee could then find the right person to lead both the Athletic Department and the football team and minimize infighting among committee members. Assuming this fast-action plan worked, it would also limit, if not eliminate, the time, energy, and effort I had been spending on intercollegiate athletics. I checked my calendar over the past three months and found that almost a quarter of my time was devoted to athletics, which was far too much, especially as the academic planning process was now going full throttle and the fundraising campaign was getting underway. I knew the next six months would be hell.

The first group MacGruger and I met were students—the captains from each of our twenty-two teams and the chair of the student council. All of them had been elected by their peers, so I thought it would be tough for other students to complain. I did not tell them that we planned to choose two of them for the search committee, though some may have guessed that. What I should have expected was a torrent of complaints from the team captains of virtually all the sports except football that their programs had been shortchanged by Knowland—since that was what I had heard from their coaches. And that was exactly what I did hear. Almost all of them had some horror story about their teams needing something, such as a bus to take them to an away game or a piece of equipment that had broken. Knowland had generally ignored these needs, apart from those of the football team.

The most helpful comments were from the chair of the student council, a Native American woman named Oneida Appletree. She was a tall, lean, handsome woman with a long black braid hanging down her back and a warm and assured manner as she spoke. She waited until I had heard a slew of complaints from team captains and then volunteered that intercollegiate athletics should create a spirit of togetherness and belonging on the campus. But this did not happen, she said. It should not be hard to develop that spirit, she argued, if team home events were scheduled on different days, were well publicized, and particularly if different dorms on campus were encouraged to be cheerleaders for different teams. Faculty should be urged to take on the same roles, she argued. "Competition is fun," she said, "particularly when the whole campus is involved." And she had an array of other good ideas, including an invitation from Emma and me to all the team captains and coaches to join us in an ice-cream party in our home. She had talked about these ideas with her executive committee and was sure the student council could help make them happen.

MacGruder and I were clear even before Oneida finished talking that she would be one of the two student representatives. We debated about the other for a while and then decided we had to choose the captain of the football team, Jamel Arnold. He was a linebacker and, no surprise, really big at about six foot two and about 220 pounds, though I never checked. As a Black student athlete, I assumed Arnold must have realized how resentful other Black players were about the strands of racism in the ways the Athletic Department operated. I also assumed he must have been a fan of Knowland, but in other respects, he seemed a reasonably sensible young man. When he spoke at the meeting, it was to say he hoped the new athletic director would support all the sports at Nebraska State the way Knowland had supported football. He certainly did not have to say that, though he probably did so in part to please the other captains. But at least it was a comment that I could support.

Selecting the faculty to invite to a meeting proved more troublesome than I expected. Choosing the past and current faculty athletic representatives was obvious. But we could not figure any easy way for us to pick other faculty without causing some tensions among those not chosen. So I turned to the deans of the schools and asked each to choose two faculty members, one woman and one man. Two of the deans, in engineering and social work, resisted saying they had no idea whom to pick. I told them that they could use any procedure they wanted. In retrospect, this was a mistake, because they asked for volunteers from their faculties. The volunteers were faculty members who had significant gripes about intercollegiate athletics at Nebraska

State. The deans selected those who were most vociferous in clamoring to be chosen.

When we gathered, I explained the search process in general terms. For the next hour, I had to listen to an explosion of complaints about the Athletic Department particularly and intercollegiate athletics at Nebraska State generally. Several urged that we drop intercollegiate athletics completely and just have club sports. Others were mad about how much money the university spent on sports, often implying that the funds would be better spent on them.

This sorrowful plea came from the chair of the German Department: "We have seventeen faculty members—all of them underpaid. Our department is on life support. Money for athletics would be better spent on keeping our department from disappearing." I knew that German had once been a popular major because many German immigrants came to Nebraska in the nineteenth century, and college students often wanted to know the language of their ancestors. But only a small handful of students were majoring in German, less than the number of faculty.

After the meeting, MacGruder and I decided we needed some neutral principal in choosing the two faculty members, or that decision could easily become contentious among the faculty. On that basis, we chose the two faculty athletic representatives before MacGruder. Fortunately, one was a woman and one a man. Each had served for a short time before MacGruder, who had been faculty athletic representative for eight years. So we chose Isabella Martinez, the chair of Latin American Studies, who had previously complained to me that her department was underfunded, and Roland Pease, chair of the Math Department. Martinez was a tiny woman with gray hair, along with a big smile and a sharp tongue. She wore large colorful hats everywhere—indoors and outside. Pease looked like a caricature of a nineteenth-century English academic, with a tweed sports coat that had leather patches on the elbows and what appeared to be a prep-school tie.

Pease was a particularly troublesome faculty member. He had been in his position for over a decade, though I had pressed all deans to encourage turnover of faculty department chairs at least every five years.

The dean of the School of Arts and Sciences claimed that no one else in the department would volunteer for the job except Pease. After we had worked through the issues of faculty productivity, the trustees had asked for a listing of the published research of every tenured faculty member on the grounds that it was their responsibility to have oversight on faculty productivity, even though we had developed a plan to deal with the issue. It turned out that Pease was one of those faculty members who taught only one course a year. Further, he had not published a single article, let alone a book, or even given a presentation at a scholarly meeting in the last decade.

Pease had gotten under my skin on another matter. Students at Nebraska State were required to take advanced algebra unless they had done so in high school. Over the years that I had been teaching courses on banking, I became convinced that what college graduates most needed was a solid course in statistics. Almost everything we read about in the news, especially in terms of politics and the economy, was full of charts and statistical analyses. Unless one had a basic grounding in statistics, it was all too easy to accept false or misleading analyses. Correlation presented as causation was one example.

So I pressed the Math Department, through Pease, to allow students—apart from those in engineering, the sciences, and some of the social sciences—to take an introductory statistics course instead of advanced algebra. He would have none of it, arguing algebra was the best mental training one could have. That reminded me of being forced to take Latin, which I disliked, because it was said to be good training for writing and speaking English. I was convinced this was a silly argument. The best training to improve one's English was to take courses in writing and speaking English. But Pease was adamant, and his Math Department colleagues went along with his views on the grounds, I suspect, that he might resign in protest if he lost, and no one else wanted to chair the committee.

To add to these difficulties, a trustee, Preston Anchor, one of the three former Knowland football stars on the board of trustees and someone who perpetually seemed as though he had just eaten a bad meal, decided to make an example of Pease for never publishing.

Anchor had been a star defensive lineman in his day and still held the record for the most NS stars on his helmet. As I mentioned, Knowland awarded those stars for outstanding, bone-crushing tackles. But now Anchor had a huge belly that hung over his belt like some half-deflated balloon. At a public trustees meeting, Anchor talked at length about the "lax standards of faculty productivity" and used Pease as his poster child. Pease was furious that this happened and angry at me for failing to defend him. While I had said publicly that I was sure he had his hands full as department chair, I could not refute Anchor's data that showed most other department chairs taught more and published more. I knew Pease would be a pain on the search committee, but I did not know how to keep him off without causing another set of problems.

We turned next to alumni, whom we suspected would be the most troublesome group of all. We were only partially right. Most of those we invited gave thoughtful suggestions. But there were exceptions. The most helpful was the president of the Nebraska State Alumni Association, Betsy Robbins, a lovely, soft-spoken woman who had been a longtime alumni volunteer in a range of programs and was always upbeat and helpful to the university. She had a radiant smile that seemed to create a kind of sparking halo around her head whenever she talked. She did not speak often in alumni gatherings, but whenever she did, I and everyone else in the room listened with care.

We also included Peter Zanza, the head of the Twelfth Man Club, which raised money to support football at the university. He was a large, overweight man with a belly almost as large as Anchor's. He had been a fullback on a Nebraska State team and seemed never to have grown past that experience. Zanza had been among Knowland's most ardent sycophants and had been writing—since I became president—blistering letters to the local newspaper blasting me for inadequate support for the football program. When Knowland died, Zanza increased the temperature of his blasts at me to the boiling point, calling for my immediate resignation.

"Why include Zanza?" MacGruder asked. My answer, I responded, was the same as that of President Lyndon B. Johnson when asked why he didn't just fire J. Edgar Hoover. LBJ said, "It is probably better to have him inside the tent pissing out than outside the tent pissing in." And that was how I felt about Zanza. I was not sure whether we would include him on the search committee, but that decision did not have to be made until after we saw how he behaved in the group lunch.

The rest of the invited alumni included some supporters and former players of a number of sports, many of whom, I knew, were both jealous and irritated at the way football had been privileged under Knowland's virtual dictatorship. And we added a few alumni who were strong university supporters but not involved in intercollegiate athletics. Finally, I chose a couple of alumni who had been consistent critics of intercollegiate athletics. The first was Joanna Winston, who was a square-jawed, no-nonsense medical doctor and for years had criticized the football program, citing the long-term dangers to players in terms of their health, particularly concussions and traumatic brain injuries. She wrote a letter to our alumni magazine listing twenty-seven former players who had terribly debilitating effects. Five of them had committed suicide.

The second alumnus, Andy Anderson, was one of Nebraska State's few Rhodes Scholars, and he went to Oxford for two years, where he played rugby. Anderson was a pharmaceutical company chemist. Hewas brilliant and wanted to be sure everyone knew that. He was stunningly handsome and seemed to walk around a room trying to be sure everyone knew just how good-looking he was. He was equally vocal about the university's failure to recognize rugby as an intercollegiate sport. His constant refrain was that rugby was the best teacher of team collaboration among all sports.

At the end of our lunch with the group of alumni, MacGruder and I talked briefly and concluded that it made sense for us to include Peter Zanza on the search committee, so he could not complain publicly about its composition. We added Joanna Winston in hopes she would be a counterweight to Zanza and they might cancel each other out. We were sorry not to include Betsy Robins, the level-headed leader of the alumni association, but we had no extra room.

Next, we turned to Athletic Department coaches and staff. MacGruder and I had lunch with a group of twenty-two representing eleven coaches and eleven staff members. MacGruder and I had hoped that the search committee could include a total of two persons from both groups rather than two from each, but during the lunch, we quickly concluded that this would not be possible. The staff members were made up of trainers, equipment managers, and office personnel, and they reflected very different views within the group. Their views often differed sharply from those of the coaches. The divisions were sharpest between women's and men's sports. They all began—before listing their gripes—by saying how much they loved the university, and I really believed they did. But they also thought the university could do better. And most of the time, I thought they were right.

A number of the trainers, men and women, said they often were not treated with dignity by the coaches, especially Knowland. "Whenever we have a meeting," said one woman, "a coach always tells me to make coffee for the group." "The coaches routinely yell at us," said a male trainer. "If a player is not in shape, we get the blame," said another.

The most troubling concerns were expressed in only slightly different language by a half dozen women. I said at the start of the luncheon that I knew, apart from that gathering, that some of the women staff members in the Athletic Department had allegedly been sexually harassed. None of them pressed charges—most likely, I thought, because they feared retaliation by Knowland. So that issue was not a surprise. But there were multiple other complaints. "There is a 'good old boys' locker room atmosphere most of the time," was how one stated the problem. "I have heard comments about my breasts and my butt more times than I can count. They are said just loud enough for me to hear them." The women coaches also had complaints, most of them were directed at Knowland, and literally all of them spoke of the toxic atmosphere in the Athletic Department when he was director.

Based on what we heard, MacGruder and I chose the coach of women's soccer, Ruth Stein, and the assistant football coach, A. J. Lederer, for the search. Stein was a quiet, stocky woman, with a look of firm determination almost always on her face. Lederer was a lean, handsome Black man with a wide smile and an easygoing manner. Both Stein and Lederer seemed level-headed and sensible, without major axes to grind. And we selected Lester Lippo, the strength trainer among the male staff, and one of the physical therapists among the women staff, Angel Samson, who was also Black. Samson had a happy-go-lucky air about her and had the nickname "Magic Fingers" because of her abilities to bring back athletes to top form. Lippo, on the other hand, looked like a Greek god, with a beautiful body—all muscle—and a reputation for pushing athletes right up to the breaking point in terms of bench presses and other grueling exercises.

We turned finally to what I thought would be a tough task—finding two athletic directors from conferences other than our own, who would be willing to join and give their best judgments to the search committees. Ideally, at least one would be, or at least have been, a football coach. Much to our pleasant surprise, the task was much easier than we had feared.

I was on one of my regular bimonthly calls with the six other presidents of our conference. Often, I found, those presidents were the only people, other than Emma, with whom I could be completely frank about a problem I was having. And the others felt the same way. They were usually full of wise counsel. Even when they were not, they were sympathetic to whatever crisis one of us was facing. We were rivals in athletics, of course, so I was a bit hesitant to seek their aid on this issue. But I decided they might be helpful, and I would lose nothing by trying.

We had a monthly Zoom call, and the next was just two days away. On the call, I told the other presidents about my desire to identify two athletic directors who would understand that I wanted a strong new athletic director / football coach who did not abuse players or anyone else. They all laughed, for they knew well what a pain Knowland had been in my life until he dropped dead at a football game, an event that immortalized him to his fans. Then they kidded me about Knowland and then about his successor. I had thought briefly of asking them if their athletic directors could serve on the committee, but I realized that this would involve too much potential conflict of interest. Several offered to talk with their own athletic directors and get back to me with some possible names.

Within a few hours, Sarah Overland, president of Utah State and my closest friend among the other conference presidents, called me and said her athletic director had suggested two terrific athletic directors—Ron Savage, athletic director at Oklahoma State, and Carlos Castro, athletic director at Minnesota State. Overland told me that his athletic director stressed that both were savvy professionals who had been in their jobs for more than a decade and did not scream at anyone, at least outside their locker rooms. And Castro was not only athletic director but also football coach. I checked their backgrounds as best I could online, and both seemed like good bets. If they did not work out, I thought, I would have had little to lose.

So I immediately called the presidents of Oklahoma State and Minnesota State and said I would like to ask their athletic directors to serve on the search committee. The president of Oklahoma State expressed nothing but admiration and enthusiasm for his athletic director. The president of Minnesota State sounded much more ambivalent about his athletic director and football coach, who had preceded the president in coming to Minnesota State. Both presidents said they would be willing to encourage these two to join the search committee if—and only if—I would promise not, under any circumstances, to steal one of them to be my new athletic director and football coach.

I agreed and asked these presidents to alert their athletic directors about the request that would be coming and to indicate it had their approval to accept. Also, I stressed that the inclusion of these two athletic directors should not be mentioned to anyone until the public announcement. The next day, I called both, and both accepted on the phone. They seemed to like the idea of being on the other side of an interview table from where they were used to sitting.

When I talked with Carlos Castro, athletic director at Minnesota State, he did raise a possible concern. "I'm pleased to join the search committee," he said. "It should be fun. But there is an outside possibility that I'll have a time conflict during the search. My wife, Sofia, is an artist," he told me, "and she shows her paintings at different galleries around the Midwest. Whenever she has a show, I go with her to help hang her paintings and to give her moral support. It's tough to see people come in a gallery, look at your paintings, and then watch them leave the gallery without buying. But I very much doubt this will be a problem in terms of the search."

"That's a small world," I responded, "because my wife, Emma, is also an artist and works part-time in one of the two Catherville galleries. I hope one day they can meet." I already liked Castro because we both had spouses who were artists and because he was frank in raising the possibility of a time conflict.

In choosing two athletic directors, I was prepared for some complaints from within our Athletic Department and perhaps from alumni as well—complaints that Nebraska State should be able to handle its own problems without calling on outside athletic directors, though I had no idea the issue would be as explosive as it turned out to be.

The next step was to call each of the proposed search committee members, one at a time, and ask them to join the committee. I stressed that I would charge the members with talking openly and frankly in the committee but that nothing should be leaked outside the committee room. The committee's job would be to choose the best candidate and then let me negotiate the terms of employment with that person. When and if a deal was made, I would make the public announcement without comments by anyone else on the committee.

I asked each proposed member for his or her pledge to abide by that rule. Somewhat to my surprise, two potential members balked. Peter Zanga, head of the Twelfth Man Club, was one, and on reflection, I was not really shocked as the voice he most liked to hear was his own. He told me he could not "in good conscience" keep silent if he thought the search committee was going off in a direction that he could not support. Given what he said, I had no choice but to thank him for his honesty, and say he would not be on the committee.

Joan Winston was the other potential member I had chosen, and what she said did surprise me. "As I've reflected on the matter," she announced to me, "I just cannot serve on that committee. As you know, I am convinced that the university is complicit in the deaths of scores of football players who get concussions, and the search committee will be seeking a new athletic director who will try to build up the football program as well as the programs of other sports. I just cannot be part of that execution squad." I said I respected her position and agreed she should not participate, given her views. I knew even before we finished the call that I would ask Betsy Rollins, head of the alumni association, to join the search committee. To my relief, when I called her, she immediately agreed.

Then I decided it would be best to choose a trustee to replace Peter Zanga. Zanga would have been a pain inside the committee, and now he would be a pain outside the committee. But so be it. I debated about not making the obvious choice, one of the three former football players, but then decided I had to do that if I had any hope of the search result being accepted by those former players. So I chose Samuel Tyson, who on issues other than athletics always seemed a steady supporter of the university and of me. I talked the matter over with Emma and the chair of the trustees, Franklin Adams, who agreed with me about Tyson. Tyson was a short, steely-haired man, built like a bulldog. He had managed to stay in shape though more than a decade had passed since he was a star halfback on a Knowland team. Tyson shortly afterward accepted my request that he join the search committee.

The day after I had talked with Tyson, I got an "urgent" call from Peter Zanga. "I have wrestled with this all night," he said, "and have concluded that it is just too important for me to be on the search committee, to protect Nebraska State football and its future. So I will accept your invitation to join the committee with the understanding that I will not reveal anything that goes on during committee meetings." I was stunned into silence while I thought what to do. If I told him I had already chosen a replacement committee member, I knew that would infuriate him and make him even more dangerous in terms of the press and die-hard football fans. So, after a long pause, I replied, "I am delighted, Peter, and know you will be an invaluable member of the committee." I had just added another member to an already-large committee and wondered if this was a sign of a rocky road ahead. It was.

When I called the other prospective members, some asked who else would be on the committee, but I told all of them that I could not say until the list was complete. Fortunately, the others all accepted, though it took three days. I had thought of asking MacGruder to make these calls but, in the end, decided that it would be more likely that they would accept if the invitation came from me. I knew the search would take time, and this might make some hesitant to agree.

We announced the search committee members on the Nebraska State website as well as in the local papers. We explained why we thought it important to have the wisdom of the two athletic directors from other campuses. For a day, I heard no reactions and thought that perhaps conflict had been avoided. But then there was an explosion of negative reactions to the choice of the two athletic directors.

A number of our coaches wrote an open letter to me claiming that choosing those two would enable them to learn the "secrets" of their coaching plans. I responded by asking for examples of what "secrets" they had in mind, and this seemed to stop that line of complaint. MacGruder told me after a few days that the coaches who wrote the open letter were just mad that they were not chosen to be on the search committee and used this excuse to vent their anger. But some alumni picked up the complaint and said it was demeaning that the university did not have enough ability within its own community to handle the search. In two days, however, things seemed to have settled down, and I asked MacGruder to organize the first meeting of the search committee.

Finally, I thought to myself, with the search committee chosen and MacGruder in charge, I could turn my full attention to the mountain of university issues that faced me.

8

November 30 was my fortieth birthday. We had my favorite dinner of meatloaf, brussels sprouts, and corn on the cob, along with vanilla gelato for dessert and, of course, a birthday cake—carrot, my favorite. I was surprised with a gift of dance lessons from Emma. We loved to dance together since we met but never managed to learn any of the South American dances, and this would be our chance. Our girls gave me a new basket and lights for my bike. I had always enjoyed riding my bike. The pedals were adjusted to take account of my right leg being shorter than my left one.

Since I became president, every Saturday morning when we were on campus, Emma and I took a long bike ride and then had a picnic in the nearby rolling hills. Sometimes we would invite a couple of students to join us—students who led one of the civic service projects on the campus. Encouraging student civic work has been a priority for me from the start of my presidency. Our campus Civic Engagement Center sponsored a wide range of activities like tutoring kids, cleaning up public parks, and serving in community kitchens. More recently, I had been encouraging more attention by the center to preparing our students with the knowledge, skills, and attributes to be engaged actively with public-policy issues and politics. I had become concerned that our politics was becoming increasingly polarized in Nebraska and throughout the country. I wanted our students to have a role in bridging the troubling political divide.

The girls were just bringing out the cake festooned with burning candles. They, along with Emma, sang "Happy Birthday" and then called on me to blow out the candles. Just as I took a breath, the phone rang on my unlisted number. I have two phones—one my personal cell phone and one a landline in our home with its number publicly listed. Calls on the landline went directly to an answering service. Polly Porter checked the calls on that line every morning and answered those that were not crank calls. I got plenty of those. She was incredibly efficient. She was a single mother with a young daughter, deaf since birth, and she managed my office with calm dispatch. Only my senior staff knew my cell phone number, and they also knew not to call me except in an emergency. Otherwise, they sent me a text if they needed to reach me. So when my cell phone rang, I knew it was important.

It was MacGruder, and he asked if he could come to see me on an urgent matter. I had been planning to call him to hear his plans for bringing the search committee together and starting the search. I could not imagine what had happened to trigger his call, but I assumed it was bad news. And it was—worse than I could have imagined.

MacGruder told me that after much soul searching, he had decided to leave Nebraska State for a position that, he said, "I just could not refuse." He described a new Institute of Technology and Innovation that was being created at the University of Texas at Austin, funded by a consortium of major corporations, including Google, Apple, Microsoft, and more. The institute would be a research-intensive entity that also provided graduate education in advanced fields, such as artificial intelligence and machine learning. A search firm had contacted him a month ago to ask him to interview for the position. The University of Texas president and the institute's corporate sponsors wanted a leader with a strong background in both engineering and technology, one who had proven leadership skills. MacGruder was a natural for the job. The search process went quickly, and he had been offered the job that day. He would start on July 1. His compensation package almost doubled his current salary and gave him the opportunity to spend literally hundreds of millions of dollars in support from the sponsors.

I was devastated by the news. With a good deal of pleading by me, MacGruder reluctantly agreed to stay on as interim athletic director for the rest of the six months while the search was underway but with the firm understanding that he would not chair the search committee as we had planned. I could not say anything else to him other than that I totally understood his reasoning, was enormously grateful for all he had done, and wished him well in his new position.

It was clear to me even before MacGruder finished talking that I would have trouble finding a new chair of the search committee. "What are your suggestions for a new chair?" I asked MacGruder.

"I was afraid you would ask that question," he responded. "I really do not have any good ones. I cannot see any of the search committee members doing the job. But what about Betsy Robbins, head of the alumni association?"

"She's a lovely human being," I said, "but just not tough enough to herd the cats we have chosen as committee members." He reluctantly agreed. "Let's both think about the matter and talk tomorrow," I said.

"What a hell of a way to celebrate my birthday," I told Emma and the girls. As I reflected on the matter, I knew that as soon as MacGruder made a public announcement about his departure or word leaked out, I would be deluged with calls telling me whom to select. I was particularly worried that Peter Zanza would rile up the football fans to demand a replica of Knowland, which is just what I did not want.

At eight o'clock the next morning, I called Franklin Adams, the trustee board chair. He was tied up when I called but called back as soon as he could. When I told him the problem, he let out a big sigh. For the next hour, we reviewed possible replacement leaders of the search committee. We first talked through the members of the search committee and quickly rejected each one as lacking the savvy needed to handle the ego-intensive members of the committee, let alone the pressures from the media, alumni, and others who would be clambering for their candidates to be athletic director and football coach.

We then considered a host of others in various categories—administrators, faculty, and alumni. Each one who seemed to have some of the qualities needed clearly lacked other qualities that were essential. Our general counsel, Norman Oreland, for example, was brilliant—my administrative staff nicknamed him "Legal Eagle"—but he had no background or experience in the world of intercollegiate athletics, though he was a person who combined good sense with strong leadership abilities.

The vice president for finance and administration, Peggy Sandstone was also an effective leader, a savvy analyst who knew how to handle tough problems with a minimum of risk, and she had a passion for intercollegiate athletics. But I had put her in charge of handling the financial arrangements for Knowland's family, and those had turned very contentious since the family wanted a much larger amount—"in recognition of his 'extraordinary service' to the university"—than the university would pay, and Sandstone was criticized in the press and by the Twelfth Man Club for being inadequately appreciative of Knowland. His widow, Wendy, threatened to sue the university and me personally, since she said I had "driven the love of my life into the grave." But in the end, we settled—a larger amount than I thought reasonable but far less than his widow had demanded.

After a full hour on the phone, checking off one prospective chair after another, Adams said to me, "I hate to admit it, but you are the only one who can do this job. It is not what you need, I realize, with both an academic agenda and a capital campaign underway. But I think you have no choice." I instantly knew he was right. But all I said was, "You may be right, but first I have to talk with Emma."

As I said that, I knew that Emma would not be happy about my taking on another burden that had maximum chances of not only causing headaches but also putting me into a swamp where I might sink. Later that morning, when we had a chance to talk, I told Emma that if I became chair, I could have some chance of finding a new athletic director / football coach who would handle all the problems that had been taking so much of my time. Otherwise, I might as well let the trustees fire me right now.

"I think you would be crazy to do this," she said. "Is there another president in the country who has headed the search for a new athletic director, let alone one who will also be football coach?" I admitted I did not know any president who had. "Just as I thought," she responded. "You have been driving yourself hard since day one as president. You have launched a big capital campaign, and you need to keep driving the academic planning effort.

"Further, you say all the time that intercollegiate athletics should not be a primary focus of your attention. And you keep repeating that the girls and I are at the center of your universe. Well, be careful, or you may find out that 'things fall apart; the center cannot hold.'" Her reference to William Butler Yeats's most famous line in his most famous poem, "The Second Coming," made me smile, and Emma snapped, "Don't laugh at me. I could not be more serious." There was a sharp edge in her voice. She was really mad—at the situation and at me.

We continued to talk for more than an hour. She was still in her bathrobe, drinking coffee. She didn't sit down once but strode up and down the living room floor. Slowly, the anger seemed to drain from her words. In the end, she said, still with some bitterness, that it was my decision. And so it was. Afterward I realized that this was probably the most heated argument we had ever had.

I called Adams later that night. And I told him it was essential that the entire board support my decision, for I knew it would be controversial. And so it was. The next afternoon he called me to say he had talked to each of the other trustees individually, and all agreed with my decision. "After all," he said, "the board members realize that they put you in a particularly tough spot, like a ship sailing in total darkness without a compass, so the least they could do was allow you to be the ship's captain."

My vice president for public affairs, Wanda Season, called a press conference for noon the next day, saying only that I would be making an important announcement. "As you know," I told a covey of reporters, who gathered in my office, "the university is about to launch a search for a new director of both the athletic department and the football program. That leader must ensure that both football and all our other sports provide the best possible experiences for our student athletes. We need a leader who is a role model of leadership for the entire campus.

"Robert MacGruder, who had planned to chair the search committee, has taken a new job at the University of Texas at Austin. When he explained it to me, how it fitted perfectly his talents and ambitions, with a heavy mind and heart, I said I understood why he could not refuse the offer. Leading the search committee is such a critical position that, with the urging of the trustees, I will be chairing the search. The proceedings of the search committee will be confidential because we will be looking for someone who, in all likelihood, already has a position at another campus that she or he enjoys. We will have no chance to attract such a person unless we can do so in confidence."

For the first half hour, I was flooded with questions from the reporters. "How are you ever going to find someone to fill Knowland's shoes?" was the first query. I silently crossed my fingers behind my back and responded, "No one could fill the shoes of that great leader," I said, "and the search committee will not try to replicate him, for he was one of a kind." That last part was true, though I did not add what "kind" I had in mind.

"You are certainly not going to consider a woman, are you, in light of the Juarez fiasco?" I knew we were not going to select a woman, for I was sure no women were or had been a football coach of a major college football team, and few were athletic directors. In response I said, "We are going to find the best person for the job." Then I added, "Associate Athletic Director Juarez did a superb job in her role while she was here. She made a mistake, a bad mistake, as she publicly recognized. She had the courage and integrity to say to everyone what happened and why she knew she had to resign. I wish all of us had that courage and integrity."

"What do you know about athletics," another reporter asked, "especially big-time intercollegiate athletics?"

There was an edge to her voice, but I responded, "When I became president, I knew little except as an avid fan. But the past two years have been an intensive learning experience. I want an athletic director who will ensure that I can go back to just being a fan and a cheerleader for all the Nebraska State teams."

Then a reporter jumped up and said in an angry voice, "Leonard Lyons, a former starting basketball player for Nebraska State who was probably headed for the NBA, and your former fraternity brother, has given me a sworn affidavit. It states that you were so mad at him that you hit him in the arm, so he could never play basketball again. Lyons asks how you can possibly expect to lead a search for a new athletic director and football coach when you not only can't play sports yourself, but you ruthlessly destroyed the career of one who could, just because you were jealous."

I was stunned. Should I explain the whole story? I asked myself. Should I tell that Lyons had tried to blackmail me? I knew the story would be front-page news in all the local media, even if I denied it. And I couldn't. I had lost my temper and done a terrible thing.

"I'll explain what happened," I said, "as soon as I clarify in my mind the circumstances that took place almost a quarter century ago." Then I turned and walked out of the press conference.

Wanda Season was at my side in an instant. "Come with me," she said sternly. We virtually ran to my office and hardly sat down when she said, "Tell me the story." I explained exactly what happened. She thought for what seemed five minutes, though was probably no more than one. Then she said, "I'm going to give you a draft statement as fast as I can. You can revise it, and we will release it within the hour." She was as good as her word.

"I made a serious mistake while an undergraduate, twenty-four years ago. Mr. Lyons and I got into an argument late one night in our fraternity house. I was drunk. Mr. Leonard Lyons probably was as well. Angry at him for mocking my limp, I hit him with my fraternity paddle, a terrible thing to do. I will be forever sorry for my misdeed. Nothing remotely like that has ever happened again."

I later learned that the reporter heard the fraternity fight story from my former friend, Jay Jacobs. After the fight, Jacobs had helped me avoid the incident from becoming public. But years later, as I have already mentioned, when I was the Business School dean and he was a professor there, I forced him to resign because he had written articles endorsing financial instruments without revealing he had been paid to do so by Goldman Sachs. The reporter tracked down Lyons and secured the affidavit. Jacobs had found an effective way to punish me at just the time when he could most hurt me.

The Lyons affair made headline stories in all the local media and included quotes from two fraternity brothers. They said getting drunk happened frequently at that time in the fraternity, and something that happened to a teenager twenty-four years ago should not be held against him. But the damage had been done to my reputation, especially as leader of the search.

In addition to the Lyons story, the sports page of the *Lincoln State Journal,* published in the hometown of our archrival, had a snide article. "You Think Sisyphus Had a Tough Job" was the headline. My statement may have kept matters from getting worse, but it did not make the firestorm of press stories disappear. I had not even started the search, and I already had a serious handicap in the eyes of the media and the public. I knew I had to put my fight with Lyons out of my mind and focus on the search.

First, however, I had to tell Emma the story of my misdeed before she learned about it in the press. I rushed home and explained to her exactly what had happened in the fraternity fight. Emma was furious. Not about the fight, as she repeatedly stressed: "That was years ago. What pisses me off is that you didn't trust me enough—really didn't love me enough—to tell me what had happened." Then she stalked off to our bedroom and slammed the door.

An hour later, Emma came back to me with a big hug. "If you are guilty of keeping a secret from me," she said, "I am just as guilty." Then she told me her secret. "During your first year as president, you remember that I took our daughters and one of their school friends to LA on a brief vacation. For the first time in our marriage, I lied to you. Rather, I didn't tell you the whole truth. Yes, the girls and I went with their friend Linda to Los Angles. And we did hear a wonderful concert and visit the amazing Getty Museum. But the real reason we went to Los Angeles was because Linda needed an abortion. Her parents are strict

Catholics and would never have agreed if asked. And Linda would have needed her parents' consent to get an abortion in Nebraska.

"Amy and Abby came to me and told me the whole story two months previously,. Linda and her boyfriend got high smoking pot at a party, and they had sex without protection. When Linda found out she was pregnant, she turned for help to her best friends, Amy and Abby. The twins turned to me. I didn't tell you any of this because Linda's father is a professor in the Chemistry Department here. I thought it would put you in a very difficult situation if you were involved in the decision to help the child of a Nebraska State faculty member get an abortion, knowing the faculty member would have opposed it.

"On the other hand, when I heard Linda's story, and thought of what her life would be like as an unwed mother at sixteen, I knew I had to help her. So I called a Planned Parenthood office in Los Angeles and made an appointment. We went there right from the airport and within a few hours, Linda had the abortion and was able to rest in the hotel suite I had rented. In retrospect, I should have told you and not kept my secret nor made the girls promise they would not tell. That was a mistake. Let's both agree—no more secrets."

Emma and I just hugged each other for a long time. I realized that what had begun as a fiasco of my making—keeping my fraternity fight secret—had turned into an event that brought us even closer together, one neither of us would ever forget. I still had the search to deal with, and that had just become harder as a result of the press stories. But my marriage was much more important and had become even stronger.

9

My next step was to ask Porter, my assistant, to poll committee members to find a date for our first search committee meeting as soon as possible. She found that the earliest the committee could meet was Friday, December 7, at 5:00 p.m. I wondered immediately whether that date was an omen of troubles ahead.

I opened the first search committee meeting by thanking the committee members and asking them to say a bit about their backgrounds. Remembering names was never my strong suit, and I had drilled myself to recall all the members' names and something about them. In doing that, I wished again, as I had often done before, that I had Emma's talent to recall not only everyone's name but everything about their backgrounds and children, even when she had met them only briefly.

I first called on the trustee, Samuel Tyson, thinking it was best to give him some deference and get his views out of the way at the outset. Tyson had a hatchet face, with a nose so sharp it looked like it could stab you. He was thin and wiry, much as he must have been when he played tight end for Knowland.

"I grew up on a small Nebraska sugar beet farm," Tyson began. "I was a star football player in high school, and I paid little attention to anything else except football and girls. My coach there was a nice fellow, but he didn't care much for discipline, and even less for how well we did in our studies, as long as we could keep our grades high enough to stay on the team. I'm sure I was admitted to Nebraska State in part—probably in large part—because Coach Knowland put his thumb on the admissions scales. My life changed the day I met Coach the first day of football practice. You've heard he was a tyrant. Yes, he was that. But he was also a great coach. He shaped my whole life, who I am, and how I relate to others.

"Coach Knowland insisted we go to every class every day and demanded we have at least a C+ average if we wanted to stay on the team. My family was literally dirt-poor, and I thought in my junior year I would have to drop out of school to help my family on the farm. But Coach Knowland lent me money for tuition and even let me stay in his house for a month when I was kicked out of my rooming house near campus for failing to pay the rent. Coach Knowland also knew I expected to run my family's farm one day. He encouraged me—ordered me is a better way to put it—to attend the School of Agriculture, where I learned what it takes to run a farm in these times of uncertainty. Legislators in Omaha and Washington have failed to recognize the centrality of agriculture to our well-being as a state and nation.

"So it won't surprise you that not only am I a fan of Coach Knowland, but I also want a football coach who knows how to win, whatever it takes. I realize we also need someone who can be an effective athletic director, with the interests of all players on every team in mind. I and all the trustees want us to find that person."

Next, I turned to Oneida Appletree, president of the student government. "I am a senior majoring in history and writing my senior thesis on the ways that white settlers systematically pushed my people out of their land in Nebraska. That land was officially an Indian reservation. The slaughter of Indians by US troops occurred in the Battle of Ash Hollow in western Nebraska in 1865, two years before it became a state. I plan to go to law school next year and devote my life to improving the lives of my fellow Indians.

"I love watching football games, but over the past three years, I have been depressed that so many students and alumni seem to think football is the most important activity and the only sport on campus. I ran to chair the Student Senate on a platform to help change that atmosphere. My fellow senators and I believe the university should do everything it can to deemphasize football and promote all the other sports equally. If this happens, intercollegiate athletics can help knit the campus together into one community. We have already proposed that home events of different sports should be scheduled on different days, and different dorms on campus should be encouraged to be cheerleaders for different teams. And faculty members should be urged to do the same. I underscore again—football gets too much attention on the campus!"

Just as I was about to call on another committee member, Peter Zanza started talking. "My name is Peter Zanza, and I am a proud alumnus of Nebraska State and played linebacker on the great football team of 1975 that went successfully to the Plum Bowl, the only undefeated football team in the university's history. I now sell Ford pickups and sedans in Catherville, but my passion is Nebraska State football. I can't be quiet after that disgraceful display of disrespect for a great sport, one which for so long has had pride of place at the university.

"We lost a giant in Coach Knowland, and I only wish the current administration had showed any respect for his unique leadership abilities. I did not have the privilege of being a member of one of his teams, since I graduated before he came, but over the years we became best friends as I have worked to enhance the Twelfth Man Club and its financial support for football. I will say right now that I have no interest in supporting anyone as athletic director and football coach who does not express a compelling commitment to ensure football has its rightful place at the head of all university sports."

It was a disgusting display of arrogance, and I had to restrain myself from responding, while I also reminded myself that it was better to have this skunk inside the tent, infuriating as it was to have to listen to him. Coming on top of what Tyson said, it was perhaps only then that I realized how tough a job this was going to be.

Next, I called on Ruth Stein, the women's soccer coach. "Soccer is my passion," she began. "I love it because it is a sport for both women and men and for all ages. No matter how good you are, you can always get better. No matter how bad you are, you can always play with pleasure. Soccer is the preeminent team sport. While there are star players, of course, like every sport, no soccer team can succeed unless every member puts the team first. The game calls for athletic prowess to excel, but even more it requires the application of intellect to a complexity of possible moves—by you, by your teammates, and by players on the opposing team. Mind and body need to be fully engaged at all times, even when you are exhausted, and soccer can be an exhausting game because you are running all the time.

"We are not here to talk about soccer, I know, but rather about finding a great athletic director who will also be a great football coach. Every coach at Nebraska State could speak with the same passion as I just did about their sports. And their players and fans could as well. And that makes me convinced that it is time, past time, for the university to find ways to put all its teams at center stage, not just football, and to find a new director whose primary goal is to do just that as well as to lead our football program."

I turned next to Isabella Martinez, chair of the Latin American Studies Department. "I do not understand much about sports," she said, "but I do know that whenever I have a varsity athlete in one of my classes, he or she is away half the time, missing my classes. Each year I receive a message from the Athletic Department telling faculty members to be sensitive about the time pressures on the athletes and asking us to be flexible and understanding when they are traveling. Baseball causes my colleagues and me more trouble than any other sport. I cannot understand why our university baseball team has to play fifty-six games a year, traveling from February through May, holding spring practice in Florida, and then taking an additional two weeks for the conference playoffs. Insofar as I can tell, the team travels all over the country, which must be exhausting for the players and expensive for the university. Other sports are bad, but baseball is the worst. In my first year here, I wrote to the athletic director and asked him to be 'flexible and understanding' about students' need to learn and faculty members' need to teach. He never even acknowledged my plea, let alone answered it."

I sensed that Martinez was just warming up when A. J. Lederer, the Black assistant football coach, broke in. "That's enough," he said. "I cannot imagine that you chose baseball just by chance. You know it has the only Black head coach, and you thought it would be an easy target. I'm not going to take that. Either apologize, or I am off the committee and will not be shy about telling the press my reason."

Martinez quickly responded, "As the only Hispanic person from the Athletic Department on the committee, I certainly understand racial bigotry. I unintentionally caused offense, and I do apologize. But I do not withdraw my point about the ways that every varsity sport corrodes the campus experiences, curricular and cocurricular, that students need and deserve. I want a new athletic director who will pay attention to that real problem and solve it."

Lederer seemed mollified when he spoke. "I accept your apology," he said, "and I do understand how frustrating it must be when your students have to miss classes. I also recognize that baseball has a longer season and more games than any other sport. I can't tell you the reason because it has always been that way. But I agree it makes sense for the new athletic director to seek conference support for reducing the number of baseball games."

What a breath of fresh air that was. I said we would take a quick break. Ten minutes later we were back in session, and I called on Carlos Castro, the Hispanic athletic director and football coach at Minnesota State. He had been hired first as football coach and then promoted to become athletic director as well. This happened not long after I had chosen Juarez as the first Hispanic associate athletic director in our conference. We had not met in person. His face is scarred, and his nose broken, and I guessed from seeing him that he had a tough life growing up. He had told me when we first talked that he felt some obligation to Nebraska State for "paving the way," as he put it.

"My role," Castro said to the committee, "is to help identify the best athletic director / football coach we can possibly find. I knew this would be difficult when I agreed to join the committee. Only a small group of men—yes, they are all men—now serve in both roles, and it's not easy, I assure you. The good news is that Nebraska State is a plum job, and there should be some good candidates. But let me say a few words about what an athletic director actually does and the challenges of doing that job along with directing the football program. Then I'll ask my fellow director, Ron Savage, to fill in all the things I will have forgotten.

"First and foremost, an athletic director needs to hire the best coaches and staff he can find and sometimes to fire those who do not perform well. By that I do not mean just winning, or even primarily winning, though winning is always a lot more fun than losing. Rather, performing well means being sure the student athletes under a coach's care and supervision are growing in terms of their athletic abilities, are gaining an understanding of the importance of teamwork, and above all are developing their character as persons of integrity, compassion, and commitment to helping others.

"These days, lockers rooms, especially in football and basketball but not exclusively, are often the only places on campuses where students of color feel they have a critical number of other students who look like they do." As he said this, I thought of my own experience listening to our football and basketball players and deciding on the spot, if I survived as president, to find a way to build a multicultural facility that included both a Black Cultural Center and a Hispanic Cultural Center. "That means," he continued, "it is extra important to hire coaches and staff who represent diversity in race, gender, and ethnic background. I put that first because generally people, including most athletic directors, think first about lots of other dimensions of the role and then, at the end, say, 'Oh, and don't forget about diversity.' Well, I know firsthand that if you wait until the end, you will never get there.

"Almost certainly, someone chosen as athletic director for the first time will know next to nothing about most, if not all, sports—except one. Unfortunately, there are no really good training programs for new athletic directors—ones that will prepare them for the job." The same is true, I thought, for college and university presidents, who come to the position without the option of a good training program. "Yet an athletic director needs to be able to identify coaching talent and ability whether it is in swimming or track. And the challenge is much tougher than choosing the best athletes in those sports.

"The best coaches were generally not the best players on their teams. There are exceptions, but in my experience, most coaches were good players in one or two sports, not stars. But they were often the team captains and showed, even as students, abilities to help shape the team into a cohesive whole. And that is what an athletic director must look for—coaches who can bring a whole gaggle of adolescents together. That is true especially for team sports, like soccer, just as Coach Stein said. But it is also true for teams made up mainly of individual performers like golf, tennis, track, and swimming. Only a good coach can fuse young men or women as a team so they help each other and enable each other to perform better than would otherwise be possible."

"But isn't college football, and college basketball as well, fast becoming just about making money for the university?" asked Oneida Appletree.

"No," said Castro, "football and basketball are not just about making money. Far from it. But collegiate athletics is a business, a big business. The athletic budget at Nebraska State is $110 million. That's a lot less than the athletic budget at the University of Nebraska. But it's still a pile of money.

"This university subsidizes all club sports and, to a degree, other intercollegiate sports as well. But most of the costs of those sports are expected to be covered by men's football and basketball, including TV revenues, which are shared equally among the seven conference teams. Most athletic directors begin in that role knowing next to nothing about budgeting beyond trying to balance the books of their own households. They learn on the job. And if they don't, they quickly get fired.

"It's true," Castro continued, "that sports needs fans, and strong fan bases need to be cultivated. Money is part of that. I do not know the facts at Nebraska State, but I suspect it is like my university, where dedicated fans, most of them alumni who played a particular sport, donate substantially to that sport. But the donations do not just happen. In collaboration with the development office, a staff is needed to ensure the right care and feeding of those donors, so they will keep on giving."

At this point, Angel Samson, the physical therapist, raised her hand and looked straight at Castro until he called on her. "How can you live with yourself as football coach, knowing that a significant share of your players will be maimed for life playing for you?" I watched as Gonza and Tyler grimaced. But Castro just smiled and quietly continued.

"But they are not playing for me," said Castro calmly. "They are playing because they love the game. They care about each other and bond in ways that often last a lifetime. Many view football as the most significant learning experience of their college careers.

"Sports are important at Nebraska State, like other universities. But academics come first, and part of the role of an athletic director is to ensure that priority is maintained and that the term 'student athlete' really means something, as opposed to gladiators who happen to be students. No surprise, this is a particular challenge in football and basketball, but it is true for all sports.

"All those responsibilities become especially difficult when they are combined with being a coach as well, particularly a football coach, because among all sports, football involves the most students, the most money, and usually the most fans. As football coach, you need to focus on ensuring that your players get the best possible experiences in terms of strengthening their characters as well as having fun. You need to hire outstanding assistant coaches and staff who can work well as their own kind of team in support of the players and the coaches.

"I've found it is possible to do both jobs, but you need to be really disciplined in terms of the time and attention you devote to each. You have, of course, to be passionate about football, just as is true of all coaches about their teams. But you also have to treat all sports with an even hand, not in terms of funding—football earns more money, has more players, and should be allocated more resources. This makes it all the more important that players of other sports and their coaches feel the athletic department as a whole is treating everyone fairly. That's the goal. I'm the first to admit, I've never reached that goal. But I keep trying.

"Well, that's probably more than you wanted to know. But let me turn to Ron Savage for his thoughts."

Without my intervention, Savage started talking. He's a handsome young man, with long blond hair down to his neck and a warm smile. And I silently chuckled at the thought that Knowland would never have permitted such long hair on any of his players, coaches, or staff.

"I second everything that Carlos said about being an athletic director," Savage began, "and have only a couple of points to add. First, it's important to remember that at Nebraska State the athletic director reports directly to the president. Even at campuses where that is not the case, a close working relationship between director and president is essential."

At this point, if he had said nothing else, I knew his presence on the committee was a wise idea. But he said more.

"The president is the one who, along with the other conference presidents, sets the rules and procedures for the conference as a whole and for all the scheduling, TV, and a myriad other arrangements that must be made. It is absolutely critical that the president have confidence in the athletic director. If that confidence is lost, it's time to get a new athletic director. Similarly, if the athletic director believes that the president is not following sound policies and procedures, it's time for the athletic director to leave.

"At least at my university, and with all respect to Mr. Tyson, it is also important not to let the trustees get involved in athletics other than as fans and endorsers of the president's decisions. I have heard of too many cases when trustees thought they should be making the key decisions in the athletic arena, not the president in consultation with the athletic director."

He did not mention that my predecessor had left because of a fight with the trustees over an athletic issue—whether Knowland could be both football coach and athletic director—but I'm sure most of the committee members made the connection and realized the trustees made exactly the same decision again this time.

"I think that's all for now," he continued, "except to say that I am delighted to be on this committee. I've been the subject of searches before but never in this position."

At this point, I was feeling good about the way the conversations were going and wondered if it could last. The answer was that it did but only for a time. Next, I called on the captain of the football team, Jamel Arnold.

"I love football," he said, "and Nebraska State has given me a great education and a chance to play. And I fully support what Mr. Tyson said about Coach Knowland. He was the father to me I never had since I was raised by a single mother after my parents split before I was born, and I never knew my real father. Coach Knowland was a tough, demanding, sometimes unreasonable father. He yelled and swore at me when I didn't do exactly what he wanted me to do. He exploded in anger, sometimes over something trivial, like a helmet strap that wasn't on right. But he made me a better player than I dreamed I could be. More important, by this year, my senior year, he gave me pride in myself, something I never had before.

"One more thing. I understand the concerns that Professor Martinez expressed about baseball requiring its players to be away from campus so much of the time. In fact, my roommate is a varsity baseball player, and I can assure her that he and his teammates are able to keep up well in their studies. Coach Knowland insisted on that. And my roommate told me his coach will not let anyone on the team play unless he has at least a B– average."

I was getting more complicated pictures of Coach Knowland than I had ever imagined. That didn't lessen my commitment to find someone not in his personality mold. The comments so far had also made me realize the complexities of the two jobs we were searching for one person to handle.

Roland Pease, the faculty chair of the Math Department was next on my list, and I was sure he would be his usual cranky self. But he surprised me.

"You would not take me for an athletics enthusiast," he began. "And I wasn't. I take a long walk every morning, and that is and always has been my only exercise. But last year a friend gave me *Moneyball*, by Michael Lewis, and I became fascinated by sports statistics, especially baseball statistics. The book, as many of you must know, is about how to run the most cost-effective baseball team, and careful analysis of statistics turns out to be a key. I became so interested in that idea that I asked the coach of the baseball team, Jim Eagleton, if he would like help in engaging in the same kind of analysis that Lewis wrote about for our baseball team. He said yes, and we have been quietly doing this for the last eighteen months, though I doubt Jamel's roommate and his teammates know this. The coach told me that the team's remarkable winning record this year compared to last is due in large part to our collaboration.

"Apart from that, I hope I can help recruit an outstanding new athletic director / football coach, one who may be willing to use statistical analyses to help improve all our varsity sports."

I was stunned. Pease had what I thought was a well-deserved reputation as being a pain. Instead, I decided he could be helpful.

Next to last, I turned to our strength trainer, Lester Lippo. He had the build of a champion weight lifter. Huge biceps reached almost to his ears and hid both sides of his neck. His stomach was as flat as an ironing board, and his legs bulged with muscles that could be clearly seen though his pants. He had told me he was a rugby fan, but I had not realized how rabid a fan he was. For ten minutes he extolled the virtues of rugby—for both women and men. "If Harvard and Notre Dame aren't scared of having rugby teams for women," he argued, "why should we be? We could be the first major public university in the country to have a women's rugby team. And I know an alumna who will finance half of all the costs for at least the next five years." Lippo continued for the next ten minutes without any regard for the rest of the university's athletic program, let alone what we might need in terms of the strengths of an athletic director. He knew only one note—rugby—and he played it over and over. I soon realized he would be trouble as the search progressed. And he was.

The last committee member to introduce herself was Angel Samson. She had blond hair and a no-nonsense look about her that made clear she was an expert in physical therapy and not shy about speaking her mind. I knew Samson was particularly concerned about football because of the injuries it caused. And, indeed, she gave us a ten-minute lecture about those injuries. Pease must have been pleased because her comments were studded with statistics, though not the kind he had in mind. She painted a dark picture for any young man who played football, including, as she did so, a number of surprises to me, such as that offensive lineman was the safest position and wide receiver the most dangerous. But then she added a zinger. "Finally," she said, "let me say this directly to Mr. Lippo. I have looked at the statistics for rugby, and they are even worse than football." Then she cited a slew of statistics. "Under no circumstances should Nebraska State add that sport. It's a killer." I knew that debate was not over, but at least there would be vocal pressure against Lippo's position.

Samson then turned to another of her concerns. "I am glad to have heard the worries for the physical well-being of our athletes," she said. "It's a serious problem. You have heard that about contact sports, but I want to alert you to what I think is the most troublesome sport of all for the physical well-being of the participants—women's gymnastics. Fortunately, I have heard no suggestions of the terrible things that have gone on at Michigan State and Ohio State, where the trainers sexually abused young gymnasts. We do not have that problem, at least insofar as I know, in any sport. But, though you may not realize this, eating disorders are very common on the team. I love our university and its sports, but I stress we need an athletic director strong enough to deal with that problem."

I told the committee I would ask MacGruder to investigate women's gymnastics and see what could be done to ameliorate the situation, if not resolve it. I knew that sounded lame, but I could not think of anything stronger I could say.

"We're off to a good start," I stressed. "Please remember that everything that is said by any committee member is solely for the committee and must not be revealed to anyone else. You have all promised to abide by that rule, and it is essential we all keep that promise if we are to find the outstanding athletic director and football coach Nebraska State needs and deserves.

"We meet again next Friday to hear from three search firms that are interested in helping us. The interim director and I chose these three after reviewing the credentials of eight national search firms."

"Why do we need a search firm?" Peter Zanza said with a snarl. "Isn't that just a waste of money?"

"No," I replied, "rather we would be wasting money as well as time, energy, and effort if we did not use a search firm. We are fortunate to have on the committee two terrific athletic directors, one of whom was previously a football coach. But we do not know, among the scores of potential candidates, who might meet our needs. A good search firm will have done searches for athletic directors and coaches in the past and has contacts across the country. That firm can talk about possible candidates who are both outstanding and potentially movable.

"The search firm can also ask tough questions about each potential candidate—questions to some of those who work for the candidate and to some for whom the candidate works. We want to know, for example, what the college or university where a candidate is located will do to keep him. Too often, I have found, people are hesitant to say bad things about a candidate. They may even be delighted to get rid of the person. We need a search firm that can push, and push hard, to get the truth.

"But we also have to be aware that search firms are generally paid one-third of the first year's compensation of the object of the search, plus expenses. This means that the search firm has a strong interest in finishing a search quickly and in promoting as much compensation as possible."

"Well, at least you can tell us how much you are willing to pay the new football coach and athletic director," Zanza growled.

"No," I said again, "that very much depends on whom we want and what position that person is in. I will do the negotiation about compensation in collaboration with our general counsel. But I can say I hope to find donors whose support will make compensation not be a stumbling block." I had decided beforehand that I did not want to tell the committee more than this, though most probably knew from media sources that the figure would be in seven figures.

Then I added that we would be fortunate to identify a successful football coach who also had experience as an athletic director at a NCAA Division I or II campus. A number of current athletic directors had been former football coaches. But we could not be assured of attracting one of them, let alone someone who was currently holding both positions like Castro. In that light, I said, if we could not attract a person with experience in both jobs, our priority had to be finding an outstanding football coach with the abilities to become a first-rate athletic director as well. One could learn the job of athletic director on the job, I told the committee, just as Knowland had done. But, I stressed, we needed to be confident that our choice would also be an effective leader for all sports. I'm sure those on the committee knew my view that Knowland widely missed that mark.

I then explained to the committee the procedures I planned for reviewing applications. A dedicated and confidential internet site would be created so that all applications could be posted for committee members to read. Since we hoped for a number of applications, the search firm, in consultation with me, would make a first pass at reducing the number, eliminating those who we thought did not meet the stated qualifications or whose applications raised other obvious concerns. Then the committee would review the files of those who made the cut, with the hope of reducing the number to five or six to be interviewed. But, I added, if any committee member read an application that had been rejected and thought it deserved a hearing by the committee, that would happen.

When I asked if any committee members had questions or comments, A. J. Lederer, the assistant football coach and the only Black person among all our coaches, spoke up. "What are you going to do to ensure that persons of color are considered? There are no Black or Hispanic athletic directors or football coaches in our conference now that Juarez is gone and only a handful of Black or Hispanic athletic directors anywhere in the country."

I had thought a good deal about this and was prepared, though I later realized I should have raised the issues without being asked. "Two key steps seem to me essential," I replied. "First, we will advertise in journals that target sports generally and also journals that target Black people and those that target Hispanic people. I think this is the best we can do in terms of advertising. Second, we should make a commitment, one that I will make public, that at least one candidate who is Black and one who is Hispanic will be in the pool and among those we interview."

Zanza immediately objected. "I thought we were going to choose the best person for the job," he said. "Now you are saying that can't be a white man."

"No," I responded, "our final choice may be a white man, but too many searches have excluded women and persons of color without adequate consideration of their abilities, and this is the way we can ensure we will not be in that position."

"But I thought it was clear that the university was precluded from racial discrimination," said Zanza in an accusatory tone. "Isn't that exactly what you are planning?"

Fortunately, I had discussed just that issue with Norman Oreland, who assured me that the equal protection clause of the Fourteenth Amendment, at least as currently interpreted by the Supreme Court, did not preclude ensuring that people of color were in an applicant pool to be considered, and I said just that in my response. (I did not add that in Oreland's view the Fourteenth Amendment was adopted to preclude discrimination against Black people, and the Supreme Court had turned the amendment on its head by saying public universities had to be almost completely color blind, though those institutions were allowed to consider race as one among a series of factors in student admissions. I feared the court would soon rule even that step was unconstitutional. And it did just that in 2023.)

Zanza then said, "Well, I still do not think such a commitment is a good idea. What happens if we receive no applications from anyone who is Black or Hispanic?"

"That means," I countered, "that we have not done a good enough job in advertising the position, and we need to go back to the drawing board and do better. But let me ask if anyone else on the committee shares Peter's concerns on this matter." The rest of the committee was silent, and I then adjourned the meeting.

I had considered some other steps that in other circumstances would have been helpful but concluded they would not work in this situation. The first was to divide the committee into three or four working groups so that each group could interview candidates and make recommendations to the whole committee. But I decided the danger was that this step would enhance divisions that would offset the potential benefits. Similarly, I rejected the idea of asking teams of committee members to visit the current campuses where candidates held positions to gain firsthand views on the candidates' home turfs. Given the possibility that the press could connect such a campus visit with the name of a candidate, this seemed too dangerous.

Finally, I said to the committee, consciously repeating some of what I had said before, "Football is important at Nebraska State. It has been since long before I was a student and will continue to be long after I am gone. But its importance should not cast a shadow on the other sports, and right now I have reason to believe it does. I hope we can find an outstanding football coach who is already also an athletic director or who has the skills to learn on the job, just as Coach Knowland did. In short, we need someone was not only can lead our football program but also will find ways to enhance all the other sports as well."

One week later, the three search firms that our general counsel and I chose for interviews with the full committee had sent us materials extolling their abilities. The firms' materials were very much the same. All three had done searches for athletic directors and football coaches at major colleges and universities. I was attracted to one firm called University Search because the cover letter the CEO sent me with its materials emphasized that a firm member assisting the search would be a recent graduate of Nebraska State. But on a hunch, I asked my assistant, Porter, to check his background. She found that he was a nephew of Knowland, and I quickly decided we did not need that complication.

When the search committee met to hear the pitches by each search firm, all of us had seen their materials. Before we started the interviews, I told the committee how we would operate. Whenever a decision was needed, such as which firm to choose, we would discuss the matter and try to reach a consensus decision. If there was no consensus, we would take a straw vote. I said I expected to be guided by that vote, but I reserved the right to make a decision contrary to the majority and explain my reasons, if I thought it was important to do so.

As soon as I announced this, Peter Zanza, without waiting to be called on, spoke. "What's the point of a committee," he complained, "if you make all the decisions? That's not the way any committee I've been on operated."

I responded, "In the end, it is my responsibility to choose the new athletic director. Ordinarily, that person would then choose the football coach. But, as you know, the trustees insist that the two positions be held by one person, just as Coach Knowland did, and we are going to do our best to make that happen. You and the other committee members are there to advise me, as university rules on search committees require. In most cases—perhaps even all—I expect to follow the views of the committee. If I cannot do so, I will explain why." At that point I wondered for a minute if Zanza would again resign. But he kept quiet.

We then heard presentations by each of the search firms—twenty minutes for their presentations, twenty minutes for our questions, a ten-minute discussion among committee members, and a ten-minute break before the next presentation. The last presentation was by BBG Sports Practice, which was led by Frank Eliot, a former athletic director at Utah State University and a basketball head coach at the University of Wyoming. I thought the first two presentations were solid but uninspired. Frank Eliot's presentation was powerful and persuasive. He had been a practicing lawyer before switching to athletic searches and seemed to have just the polite but probing approach that was needed. When I asked for reactions, one committee member after another said that BBG Sports Practice was the best, and I enthusiastically agreed. It felt good that our first action was by consensus.

I told the committee that in the next week, BBG Sports Practice, in consultation with our vice president for public affairs and me, would draft an advertisement announcing the search. I would immediately circulate the ad to the committee members for their comments. And I hoped we could place the ad the following week. I also told the committee that I wanted to be able to name a new athletic director / football coach before the end of the next three months as MacGruder was leaving then. I stressed that at least a brief overlap would be extremely helpful.

The committee accepted this procedure without objections.

A few days later, Wanda Seasons and Frank Eliot showed me a draft ad to be sent to all the journals that traditionally cover intercollegiate athletics, as well as the *Chronicle of Higher Education, Inside Higher Education,* and several journals that focused on Black and Hispanic readers. I thought the ad seemed fine, though I knew the text of such ads rarely, if ever,made a difference in attracting talent. The realm of Divisions I and II intercollegiate athletics was not large, and we certainly wanted a football coach who was already an athletic director or who had the talents to become one. Virtually all the Division I athletic directors already knew, I was sure, that Nebraska State would be looking for a new leader, if only because the press coverage was so widespread about Juarez and why she left, followed by the trustees' mandate that we hire someone who could do both jobs.

I was busy as always over the next week and was pleased that none of the media reporting on the search included any of what was said at our first meeting. But I was deeply unhappy that I had to grapple with a new crisis. It involved Raymond Charter, the associate provost and a professor in the School of Agriculture. Charter and his wife were also close friends with Emma and me, and we often played tennis doubles together.

Jennings Rogers, the provost, became suddenly sick a week before classes began. He then called Charter and asked him to speak to the parents of the freshman class on the day freshmen moved into their dorms. Charter did so and gave a copy of his speech to Rogers, who was impressed by its eloquence. Weeks later, a parent—who had heard Charter speak—received a letter from a friend whose child was a freshman at a northeastern university. The friend enclosed a copy of a speech given to parents of the freshman class at that university, saying she thought it was a great speech. The Nebraska State parent sent a copy of that speech with a letter to Rogers, saying that the speech sounded word for word like the one she had heard. Rogers checked the texts of the two speeches, and they were identical. Rogers then came to me and asked what to do.

My first instinct was to ask myself whether I had to do anything. After all, this was just a talk to parents. While Charter did copy the words he used, every talk to parents involves essentially the same points, though the words differ—your child is starting a journey of exploration; there will be ups and downs, but we will take good care of that child; please do not be a helicopter parent, who hovers over the campus, watching your child; and so forth.

But as I reflected on the matter, dark clouds appeared in my head. First, I had been learning since I became president that I had to act on the assumption that the facts in this situation would become public. Every once in a while, I was able to keep something quiet, but I could not count on this being one of those cases. If and when the story was in the media, it would surely emphasize three facts. The first was that Charter plagiarized. Second, plagiarizing is a cardinal sin in academia, maybe *the* cardinal sin. And third, Charter was a close friend of mine, and I would be at least party to the decision to try to cover up the situation by saying nothing. Rogers and I spent an hour coming up with the next step. This was it.

Rogers called Charter to come to his office that afternoon, and I was there as well. Rogers spoke, but I made clear at the outset that he had my full support in what he was saying. Rogers told Charter that we knew the full facts about the speech and that Charter had two options. One was to resign as associate provost and professor, and nothing more would be done about the matter, though Rogers emphasized that the facts still might come out. The second option was to resign as associate provost and try to return to the School of Agriculture faculty but, in doing so, also write a public letter to that school's faculty, students, and staff, explaining exactly what had happened and asking the faculty to allow him to continue as a professor.

Charter wrote the letter. In it he did not try to "spoil an apology with an excuse," in Benjamin Franklin's felicitous phrase. Rather, he told exactly what happened, made clear he violated a sacred trust with his colleagues and the university community, and asked the faculty to allow him to continue in their midst but expressed understanding if they refused.

Charter sent a copy of the letter to the student newspaper, and it appeared on its front page the next day. An editorial in the paper was kinder to Charter than I had expected, saying that his acute embarrassment should be punishment enough. The School of Agriculture faculty agreed, and Charter stayed on.

Finally, I thought I had time to turn to the job for which I was hired—to strengthen the whole university. I had launched the program to develop a strong academic agenda, and now we needed to launch a major campaign to raise the funds to pay for what I hoped would be an impressive series of new academic initiatives.

10

Every once in a rare while, if one is really lucky, it seems that an angel from heaven is watching out for you either to enable you to avoid some catastrophe or to further some major goal you have set for yourself. It was my great good fortune that this happened just after I refocused on a major fundraising campaign to support the best proposals that emerged from the academic planning agenda. It would be called "Nebraska Forward" to underscore that the campaign would benefit the entire state. The Development Office had a contest among alumni donors to suggest a title, and some of the suggestion were wild—"Don't Wait, Help State," was one. I stayed out of the process, though I thought "Nebraska Forward" lacked sparkle. But when I had to choose between this title and the other favorite, "Nebraska on Top," I thought that one was even more boring.

The angel from heaven actually came in the form of three angels—Louis Rossiter and his twin brothers, Samuel and David. Their great-great-grandfather, Clarence Rossiter, who had moved to Nebraska from Utah in 1862, was the initial benefactor of the university. The brothers were raised in a strict Mormon family. All three were graduates of Nebraska State, but none had been more than modest donors to the university—except for a large scholarship fund given years ago, soon after they had all graduated. All three were billionaires.

Over time, I found out from our Development Office "development" is a euphemism for fundraising—the reason for their lack of support for the university: they could not stand my predecessor, Enzo Enrico. Apparently, they were watching the first football game of the season some years ago, before I came to teach there. Nebraska State was playing the University of Akron, and our university was ahead 44–7 in the third quarter. One of the referees called a penalty against Nebraska State, and Knowland exploded off the bench and onto the field. The referee then ejected Knowland from the game. Knowland was so mad that he pulled the entire team off the field, and Nebraska State forfeited the game. Even Knowland's supporters knew he had gone too far, and he was blasted by the media. But Enrico rose to Knowland's defense and said he had been entirely right in a press conference after the game. "Coach was just standing tall for the rules of the game," he said. "Without those rules, there is no game." This cemented Enrico's standing with Knowland. But it made the Rossiter brothers so angry that they stopped all donations to the university.

Louis was CEO of Rossiter Farms, the hog farming company his great-great-grandfather started. Louis was a big man—tall and wide—and must have weighed at least 250 pounds but without an ounce of fat on him. He also had a big smile on his sunburned face most of the time, and you could immediately tell he spent most of the day outside on his farms. Rossiter Farms was the largest company of the kind in the world when he started, and over the previous ten years, it had doubled its size to include almost a million hogs at any one time. Samuel and David earned engineering degrees, left Nebraska after graduation, and moved to San Francisco to join the world of high-tech start-ups. As identical twins, they were almost impossible to tell apart. They were both medium height and handsome. Fortunately, only Samuel wore glasses. Otherwise almost anyone would have kept getting them confused.

The three brothers each owned a third of Rossiter Farms, so they could have just retired to a beach somewhere. Instead, Samuel and David moved to Silicon Valley. They bought a small start-up, Reality Now, focused on virtual reality. In four years, and after multiple patents, Reality Now became a publicly traded company worth about $32 billion. The twins owned two-thirds of the stock. More recently, Reality Now had bought a software firm called Connect that had a platform like Zoom but also offered a wide array of means for users to interact with each other in ways not possible via Zoom. Connect was expanding rapidly into the education arena.

It was no surprise, therefore, that I set my sights on the three Rossiter brothers as a key—probably the key—to a successful fund-raising campaign. I invited them to sit in my skybox to watch football games, to stay in the president's house on campus, and to meet some of our most prominent faculty. Perhaps most useful, they knew I had been furious at Knowland. It soon became apparent that each of the three had different interests, but all three were potential high rollers for the campaign.

Louis had his own foundation with around $4 billion in assets, and the twins each had their own foundations worth several times that amount. The three brothers were extremely close to each other, though the twins lived in California. Each brother was a board member of the other brothers' foundations, and the foundations had sometimes found ways to collaborate. For example, all three foundations contributed to the Joslyn Art Museum in Omaha and other cultural attractions throughout Nebraska.

Most important from my perspective, all three foundations had joined together years ago to endow a cluster of one hundred undergraduate Rossiter Scholarships at Nebraska State. These scholarships were designed to keep some of the very best high school students in the state from leaving Nebraska to go to college elsewhere. The scholarships provided tuition, room, and board, plus funds for travel during the summer, and special seminars and programs for the Rossiter Scholars, as they were called.

A group of faculty initially resisted the idea of Rossiter Scholarships on the grounds that they were not based on financial need. But their opposition was overruled when those faculty learned that many of the state's best students who applied but did not receive a Rossiter Scholarship nonetheless decided to come to Nebraska State, which they would not have otherwise done if they had not applied for a Rossiter Scholarship and learned about the university's strengths. I recall the letter to me from a recent graduate who came even though he was not a Rossiter Scholar: "Enrolling at Nebraska State was the best decision I ever made. I turned down Yale, your alma mater, to do so. Though I didn't receive a Rossiter Scholarship, I came anyway with a smaller scholarship, wanting to stay in Nebraska, near my family. I was determined to prove I could succeed—and I did." I sent copies of the letter to the Rossiter brothers. They were so pleased that they expanded the scholarship endowment to support an additional twenty students each year.

I had talked to each of the brothers multiple times, and all three had enjoyed staying at the president's house with their wives. The first time they came, Louis brought an album of pictures of the house soon after it was built and was delighted when he saw the decor was still much the same, though the house, of course, had been modernized many times over the years.

All three brothers loved classical music, and they regularly came to master classes given by our faculty and, on occasion, by visiting musicians. One weekend, our Music School had invited two of the most renowned musicians in the world, Yo-Yo Ma and Emanuel Ax, and their concerts and master classes were captivating. As a special thank-you to Emma and me, they came to the president's house and played Beethoven's Concerto for Violin, Cello, and Piano in C, known as the *Triple Concerto,* with one of our faculty violinists. The three Rossiter brothers were our only guests for that private concert and were as thrilled as I was. Samuel Rossiter was an amateur cellist, and when I told this to Yo-Yo Ma, he gave Louis an impromptu one-on-one lesson. Samuel was over the moon.

We heard our Music School perform Puccini's *Madam Butterfly* on Friday night and Mozart's *Don Giovanni* Saturday night. Emma commented as we left the Musical Arts Center on Saturday that both operas were so misogynistic that they would have triggered angry campus protests had their beautiful music and arias not been written centuries ago. All of us agreed.

On Sunday morning, after the three brothers returned from church, I asked them to join me in my study. I think of myself as having a cool head even in tense times, but I was really nervous. The size and shape of the fundraising campaign depended on their reactions to what I was about to tell them.

I explained in some detail our initial plans for the campaign and how it was directly tied to our academic planning effort. Then I spelled out the key steps in the campaign. They seemed impressed. They particularly liked linking the campaign to enhancing academics, though I had also made clear that we had significant needs in athletics, and that would be part of the campaign as well.

"One last point," I said to them. "As you know, the reason that our athletic teams are called the Hogs dates to your great-great-grandfather. I know the nickname was intended by the university's president to honor him, but frankly, I and most Nebraska State fans and friends whom I know think the nickname is silly. The students certainly do, and the faculty I've talked with agree. But Knowland was adamant that 'Hogs' was an essential part of the university's heritage. I raised the issue with him soon after I became president, and he screamed at me that it would be sacrilegious to abandon 'Hogs.' Now that Knowland's gone, would you be offended if we found another nickname?"

All three immediately burst out laughing. "For years," Louis said, "all three of us have thought that nickname was absurd. If our hogs could talk, even they would think it ridiculous. By all means, change it."

I let out a sigh of relief and told them that my plan was to have a contest to choose a new nickname, and a fun task of the search committee for a new athletic director would be to choose the name from among those proposed by all members of the university community, including alumni.

In the next few days, I talked with each of the brothers individually. I started with Louis, the eldest. I knew he had been battered in the press—particularly outside Nebraska, but even inside the state—with sharp criticisms that Rossiter Farms was one of the largest producers of greenhouse gases in the country. For a time, Louis and Rossiter Farms made the case in ads that hogs were just a third of 1 percent of the total greenhouse-gas problem in the US. The company's public-relations firm argued that the benefits to the country and the world of the $5 billion business more than offset the costs in global warming. But the antihog publicity was getting more virulent, and protesters had been promoting a boycott of all pork from Rossiter Farms. One holding pen for hogs was even burned to the ground in the night. Posters appeared everywhere on campus with "Rossiter" in giant type above the picture of a fat hog and a big black cross on the poster stretching from corner to corner.

In response, Louis teamed up with Smithfield Foods, the country's biggest pork producer, to invest in a massive experiment to build huge ponds that held hog manure under heavy plastic covers that trapped the methane gas instead of letting it escape into the atmosphere. The gas was processed and then sent to electric power plants. Louis planned a similar effort in Nebraska, one that could ultimately meet a large share of the state's power needs. At the time, over half of that power came from coal.

Louis was excited about the prospect of the effort. "This could transform the way hog farming is seen by everyone who worries about climate change," he told me. I knew he was also interested in finding other ways to help Nebraska and its economy through agricultural innovation. Our School of Agriculture, perhaps in collaboration with the Business and Engineering Schools, was a logical focus of his interests.

Louis continued, "I have come to be terrified by the impact of climate change and am committed to finding means to grapple directly with the ways energy production is rapidly destroying our planet. I was slow in coming to this realization, but my kids have tutored me well. I now realize that what my family has done at Rossiter Farms is a big part of the problem. Just as I was coming to understand this, I learned about the Smithfield Farms experiment and wanted to share in that important work. This led me to realize that an enormous amount of the pollution caused by farms could be mitigated, and the experiment with Smithfield Farms is just one example. For more than one hundred and fifty years, providing better food and delivering it to more people was our company's sole goal. Now we have to ensure that making the planet safe for our grandchildren is equally important."

Samuel Rossiter, whom I quickly learned never to call Sammy, had been an English major at Nebraska State. He told me at length in one of our lunches over the past year that he was deeply distressed that professional undergraduate education—especially in business, education, engineering, and nursing—included over half of all the majors in colleges and universities across the country. The percentage was even higher at Nebraska State, where agriculture was second only to business in numbers of majors. Samuel realized that Nebraska State had some strong departments in the School of Arts and Sciences—especially in the humanities—but overall most departments in the school had slipped badly in the last decade. The liberal arts, therefore, was a natural place for Samuel to concentrate his giving. And he stressed that the School of Music should be included: "I believe passionately that learning to appreciate music of all types and kinds is essential to a life well lived."

He went on: "I've seen too many engineers and businesspeople who have no ability to communicate, orally or in writing. One of my favorite Nebraska State professors wrote these lines that have stayed with me since graduation: 'The statement of an idea is no less important than the idea itself. Clarity of expression can never replace thought, but no thought can be expressed with full force unless it is clearly stated. Few of us can write gracefully, but all of us can write intelligibly.' Yet over and over in my professional life," Samuel added, "I have had to deal with men and women who cannot write or speak a simple declarative sentence, which is one of man's noblest architectural achievements. They cross swords with syntax in almost every sentence."

Samuel made clear that his concern went well beyond simply learning how to communicate effectively. "I am troubled that people of all ages with whom I connect seem to have no idea of history—the history of this country, let alone the rest of the world. Their focus is a problem happening this afternoon at three o'clock, without a clue that the problem has roots in the past." He went on to praise the liberal education that he received in the Honors College at Nebraska State. "It was there that I learned much more than just critical thinking or problem solving, important as those skills are. I learned how to work with people who have fundamentally different mindsets than mine. And, most important, I learned how to think about issues in terms of who I am and how I want to relate to the world.

"The Honors College was great, but I want to make its benefits available to all students at Nebraska State. My donations will go to the School of Arts and Sciences, to enable all students in their first two years of general education to have the equivalent of an Honors College experience, and to the School of Education, to help prepare K–12 teachers for future generations of Nebraska youth. And I want that to happen at all three Nebraska State campuses, not just the main one."

David, the third brother and Samuel's twin, had suffered from prostate cancer in his early thirties, and that experience made health care his primary concern in terms of philanthropic giving. But he stressed to me that curing cancer was not where he wanted to focus some of his wealth, but rather on ways to enhance health care in rural areas.

He told me he remembered driving with his father through dozens of Nebraska small towns and the farmlands that surround them. "Over and over," he said, "I would hear stories about people of all ages who could and should have been cured but were not because they were not near a major hospital in an urban area. Given our abilities to wire the country via the internet, there must be ways to bring better health care to rural Nebraska and similar parts of the rest of the nation.

"I realize there are still pockets of the country without internet access, and Nebraska has more than its share of those places. But the same was true of rural electrification in the Depression, when federal policy changed that in 1936. I have created a grassroots lobbying group to press Congress for a rural internet access act. But that would only provide opportunities to deal with the rural health problems in this country. We need much better techniques to deliver health care via technology throughout the world. The Schools of Agriculture,

Business, Engineering, and Medicine, along with the Department of Communications, need to join together to start a new interdisciplinary institute to help make that happen. That is what I want to fund." I was thrilled by this bold initiative.

Finally, all three brothers shared an interest in Nebraska State intercollegiate athletics. Louis had played basketball for the university. Samuel had been manager of the football team, and David had been a star water-polo player. As a result, it was understandable that their interests in intercollegiate athletics differed.

I was not surprised when Samuel had told me he was delighted that Knowland was no longer neither athletic director nor football coach. And I knew Samuel's disdain was reinforced by his Mormon upbringing. Knowland's foul tongue and bullying clashed with how the three brothers were raised. I emphasized to Samuel that in attracting a new football coach / athletic director we needed someone who would be a role model for his players and other students. I said it would be an enormous benefit if we could provide a salary significantly higher than Knowland's.

At that time, the football coach at the University of Nebraska earned $3.2 million, which still seems to me an obscenely large amount. In his last year, as I wrote, Knowland was paid $1.5 million dollars as football coach and another $1 million as athletic director, along with additional payments for endorsements. More important, I stressed, our football stadium was in substantial need of renovation, and the indoor practice facilities were in disrepair.

When I talked with Louis about basketball at Nebraska State, he was not surprised to learn that the men's team earned far less revenue than its counterpart at the University of Nebraska, that the coach's salary was much lower, and that the facilities were also inadequate. We needed a new building to accommodate the basketball courts, locker rooms, and other necessary facilities. I did not have a figure in mind for a new building, but knew it would be expensive.

My talk with David about the needs in other sports flowed back and forth over all the sports at the university. He was particularly interested in helping the women's teams, but after we discussed the range of sports, men's and women's, at Nebraska State, he said, "You know, I really think I should find a way to help support them all." I was delighted.

I was feeling euphoric. In the next few weeks, the three brothers agreed in principle to support a major fundraising campaign, focused on the academic planning agenda that was underway. Each brother would direct his support toward the arena that was his passion, in both academic fields and athletics as well. Their gifts would anchor the fundraising campaign, which I had been designing with advice from Alton Fundraising Solutions and the research department of the university's Development Office.

Then a huge monkey-wrench was thrown into the plan by a long article in the *Sentinel*, the student daily newspaper on the Catherville campus. An undergraduate had written one of her history papers on the Rossiter family and in the process learned that Clarence Rossiter, great-great-grandfather of the three brothers, had gained his land at the expense of the Chano Tribe of Indians.

The student who wrote the paper sent it to the newspaper, and one of its editors began a month-long effort to dig up as much dirt as possible about Clarence Rossiter. It turned out that there was plenty.

The US government, via the army, actually pushed the Chano Tribe out of Nebraska southwest into Oklahoma in 1866, just after the end of the Civil War and before Nebraska became a state. The force behind the push was Clarence Rossiter. Whether or not he actually bribed the army's commanding officer in the territory on the one hand and Bureau of Indian Affairs officials on the other, is a subject of controversy. But it was clear from the student's research into newspapers of the time and a cache of letters in the Nebraska Historical Society that Rossiter thought Indians were inferior beings who should be forced to assimilate to the ways of white people. The best means to do that, he believed, was to herd them onto land that no white people wanted, call it a "reservation," and then force them to follow the edicts of the US government in terms of how they lived. Here's just a few quotes from one of Clarence Rossiter's letters to his wife, Faith. It was written just after Clarence arrived from Utah, where he had been a struggling farmer until he set out in a covered wagon to make his fortune in

Nebraska, leaving Faith behind until he had made enough money to build a home for her and their children:

> I am thrilled to tell you that the land where I have staked our claim is rich and fertile, with a river running through it to give us water. The Chano tribe has apparently been there for centuries. It's a small tribe, seemingly isolated from other tribes in Nebraska. As a result, with my encouragement, the Army ordered the tribe to leave or be slaughtered. Most of the tribe did leave for land that was promised them in Oklahoma, but about a dozen Indian warriors resisted, and in a pitched battle with our soldiers, all the warriors were killed. Fortunately, only one soldier lost his life. It gave me enormous pleasure to personally scalp two of the Indians and then hang their scalps in the little log cabin I have built for us. I'll start plowing this week, and soon, I hope, will have enough money to bring you and our children here.

There was more, much more, in the article run by the student newspaper, which was printed in a separate six-page special section. The image of Clarence scalping an Indian who was murdered by US Army soldiers, possibly at the direction of Clarence but certainly with his enthusiastic approval, was enough to cause a campus explosion. A petition was signed by over one thousand students, faculty, and staff demanding that the Rossiter name be dropped from the scholarship fund. If that could not happen, the large endowment should be returned to the Rossiter family.

I realized that I had to act fast. Either I could essentially accept the petition's demand, or I would have to find another route. I called the three Rossiter brothers, told them what had happened, and asked to meet with them immediately. The twins said they were in the middle of a major high-tech acquisition and could not leave San Francisco, but their company jet would be on its way shortly, and their brother Louis and I could take it directly from Catherville to the airport in Palo Alto, California, near company headquarters in Palo Alto. I said I wanted to bring Wanda Season, the university's vice president for public affairs, with me, and they readily agreed. Louis, Season, and I spent the entire flight brainstorming about what to do. As a result, we were able to meet at about eleven o'clock in the evening after I called.

I was tired when we gathered in Samuel's Atherton, California, home because it was two hours later, Nebraska time. I had never been to the house—all our discussions had been on the campus or by phone. The house was both huge and stunning. I knew it had been designed by Frank Gehry, the architect of Disney Hall in Los Angeles, and I expected it would replicate the swirling forms that mark that building. Instead, it was an austere modern home, no less than eight or ten thousand square feet on several acres of land full of live oaks along with orange and apple trees. As I walked in the front door and into a foyer, I saw a huge living room to the left with a vaulted ceiling and a small library with a harp and piano to the right. Those instruments reminded me how much all the brothers enjoyed classical music. When I walked into the living room, I glanced through the back window and saw a full-scale children's playground with every imaginable kind of slides, swings, and a carousel.

Samuel gave Season and me a drink while he and his brothers drank lemon-flavored soda water, and we sat down to talk. I had forwarded to each brother copies of the newspaper article, so they were fully prepared. On the plane, after a number of false starts, Season had suggested an approach that Louis and I agreed made sound sense, and I outlined that approach to the twins. Essentially, the three brothers would come in a day or two to the campus and hold a public session in our auditorium in which they would outline a plan and take questions and comments after doing so.

In essence the plan was relatively simple. Louis, as the eldest brother and the one now in charge of the farm and land that was the focus of the protests, would tell those at the session that he and his brothers had not known about the massacre in which their great-great-grandfather had a primary role and that they were as shocked and upset as were those who signed the petition. He would then say that the three Rossiter families had two options. Wanda had written out a script, though we all expected that Louis would put it into his own words.

"We could take back the scholarship endowment," he would say, "and not give any further donations to the university on the grounds that Rossiter money is tainted. If that happens, we will find other institutions, very likely including other universities, to invest our funds, with particular attention to the systemic racism that has so oppressed Indians since the founding of our country. We would do that with heavy hearts because Nebraska State is dear to our minds and hearts. It gave us great educations, and we want to support it.

"There is another option, but we will take it only with the support of the Nebraska State faculty. The president of the university supports this other option, but the faculty is the lifeblood of the university, and without the endorsement of the Faculty Senate, we could not go forward with the second option. What is that option? We would ask ourselves, how we could best use a large share of the monies that we three brothers have, in major part thanks to Clarence Rossiter? Each of us has worked hard to multiply the funds that we inherited, just as our parents did. But we do not seek to avoid the reality that Clarence Rossiter provided the inheritance that enabled us to do that.

"The second option is that together our three families will invest a total of five hundred million dollars in Nebraska State University. Those funds will not make up for the slaughter of Indians over a hundred and fifty years ago. But this investment will be an acknowledgment of the wrong that was done. The university and its leaders will decide how our funds will be allocated within the arenas of each of our interests, with one key exception. One share of the monies must be used to support a new Native American Studies Center, funding for new faculty positions in Native American studies, and scholarships to support Native American students."

Then Louis would outline the interests of the three brothers and say that each would plan to invest $150 million in the parts of the university that we had discussed. Louis would make $100 million of his gift for new programs focused on climate change, to the School of Agriculture, working in collaboration with the Schools of Business and Engineering. Samuel's gift of the same amount would be to the School of Arts and Sciences and the School of Music to help ensure that all Nebraska State students would gain a first-rate liberal education, whatever discipline they majored in. And David's gift of $100 million would be to the School of Medicine to promote ways to enhance the delivery of medical care to rural areas in the US and around the world. In addition, the three brothers would each contribute $50 million for a new Native American Studies Center, hiring faculty in Native American studies, and scholarships for Native Americans from Nebraska. Finally, all three brothers would together donate $50 million to support strengthening intercollegiate athletics at Nebraska State. The donation from Samuel would be for the football program, and the donation from Louis, for the basketball program. With a little prodding from me, Louis had agreed to include women's as well as men's basketball. David's donation would be for the other sports, with an emphasis on strengthening the club sports.

Just as Louis finished outlining the plan, Samuel and David together said they adamantly opposed it. "We didn't agree to make our contributions to Nebraska State as blood money for the sins of Clarence Rossiter," David said. "We didn't slaughter any Indians. Why should we be held responsible for what our ancestor did more than a century ago? And he didn't kill the Indians—United States soldiers did that. We are trying to help Nebraska State, and for this we get a kick in the pants! Why don't we just go to some other university that will be glad to have our donations?"

Samuel, nodding in agreement, said, "David and I made our money in Silicon Valley on our own. Sure, we had our shares of the hog farm as collateral for what we borrowed. But we built our business, not Clarence Rossiter. We shouldn't be blamed for his misdeeds. Besides, that was a very different time. Remember, Andrew Jackson had finished two terms as president not long before Clarence arrived in Nebraska. Jackson had led brutal campaigns against Indian tribes that required the Creek Indians to surrender vast territories in what is now Alabama and Georgia." And pulling out a twenty-dollar bill picturing Jackson, Samuel added, "And now our country views him as a hero." Both brothers went on to say in a dozen different ways how upset they were to be blamed for what happened more than a century earlier and to be told that the money they would give to Nebraska State would be to atone for their family sins, not as charitable contributions.

I watched Louis carefully, as he said, "Let me think about this." He seemed in pain. I knew his twin brothers looked up to him and hoped he could find some way forward. After what seemed an hour but was probably only ten minutes, he spoke. "I understand your points. The country has changed since the days of our ancestor, and we are certainly not responsible for what he did. Nonetheless, we three did benefit from his actions. This is a tough problem that deserves to be viewed from all perspectives.

"I have a suggestion. We are the senior Rossiters, and we can make the decision about this. But our children also have a stake in how the issue is resolved. Each of us has three children, and each of us has included those children on our foundation boards because we think they should have a say in Rossiter charitable giving. They are the future.

"I think we should have a video call with our children on the line to talk the situation over. Of course, we should use your internet platform, Connect. I suggest we ask Wanda Season to write out the background and the proposal, which I support. We'll send the proposal out later today, asking our children to consider the matter and be prepared to discuss it during an urgent conference call at noon Pacific time tomorrow. We'll probably not get everyone, but we will at least learn more by doing this."

I could tell that David and Samuel were torn. They loved and respected Louis, as the leader of the family and the one responsible for the hog farm, which brought substantial dividends to themselves and their children. But they were also irritated by what they viewed as self-righteous faculty and students who wanted to erase ugly events in American history—events that helped make the country prosperous.

After some reflection by both Samuel and David, they turned to each other, smiled, and then said OK at the same time. I won't go into the details, but Season drafted the proposal and showed it to all of us within an hour. Louis wrote a cover letter explaining the urgency of the matter and why the call the next day was so important. All three brothers signed the letter.

The next morning at noon, Louis, with Samuel and David at his side, opened the session and recapped the situation and the proposal that he supported. He turned to the twins and urged them to express their views. They had obviously checked signals with each other beforehand, and Samuel said they would first rather hear from all their children. Eight of the nine children joined us via video. The children all introduced themselves to Season and me. Five of the eight were in college, though not Nebraska State, and two of the others were in graduate school. One was working for a company in San Francisco.

Sarah Rossiter, one of the oldest, said she would speak for all the children, who had talked about the matter for the previous two hours and had come to a consensus. She underscored they all appreciated being asked their views. She said they were unanimous in believing that the proposal should be accepted.

"We understand that we and our parents were not responsible for how Clarence Rossiter obtained his land. But if this proposal is rejected by our family, we also understand that for generations to come, Nebraska State students will know that the place where they are studying was stolen from Indians whose blood drenched land that is now the campus. This is bound to have a troubling impact on most of them, not just those who are Native American. It has that impact on us now that we know the facts. And it may even keep prospective students from coming to Nebraska State.

"This proposal offers a way forward that, if accepted by the Nebraska State faculty and trustees, will help offset the damage done all those years ago. It will say to the entire university community that the Rossiter family is dedicated not only to strengthening Nebraska State but also to enhancing the numbers of Native American students on the campus and creating a new Native American Studies Center. We, as a family, need not then hang our heads in shame. We can be proud of what we have done to help ensure the Rossiter family will be seen as doing so much good rather than just causing the bloodshed of innocent Indians."

The video screen was silent for several minutes. Then David smiled at Samuel and said, "I guess we just got outvoted." That quickly, the plan was approved by the three brothers and their children.

Louis indicated that in talking to the university community via video, he would follow exactly the script Wanda had written. "She's a much better wordsmith than I am," he said. This would involve the largest single contribution ever made to a public university, $500 million. The gifts of the Rossiter brothers would be the anchor of the large fundraising campaign that I had been designing with advice from Alton Fundraising Solutions and the research department of the Development Office.

At Season's suggestion and with my approval, the brothers agreed that the gifts would be announced as based on raising matching money. Two dollars of matching money would have to be raised for every dollar of money from the Rossiter brothers. This would give a real incentive for others to donate toward our campaign goal of $1.5 billion. But the brothers privately assured me that the university could count on their gifts however much matching money was raised.

The three brothers, Season, and I discussed this plan and exactly how best to frame the two options over the next six hours. It was almost dawn when we were finally done. I had been worried during the entire time we had been talking that a campus meeting where the brothers would talk would too easily turn into a circus with no one able to speak because of continuous and boisterous protesting. I had visions of what happened at the University of California at Berkeley when that university had to spend $250,000 for security when a very conservative commentator was on campus to speak.

I had long thought that it was important for students on a campus to hear differing views, but I believed there was no First Amendment requirement that the speakers actually be on campus. Then Season had an inspiration. She suggested we link via the internet the Rossiter twins in San Francisco and Louis in Catherville to the auditoriums on the Catherville campus and the two regional campuses. We could again use the twins' internet platform, Connect. I would open the session, Louis would speak as planned, and then students and others could both listen and ask questions or make comments to the brothers or me, but the dangers of disruption would be minimized.

The Rossiter twins were delighted not to have to make a trip across the country, though they had said they would have if it were necessary. And Louis was pleased to stay on his farm. Season said she would make the required arrangements along with publicity about the meetings in the three auditoriums, without making it public that the brothers would be speaking from other locations.

The three brothers went to sleep in a couple of the bedrooms in Samuel's home, while Wanda and I went to a nearby hotel, whose desk clerk was shocked to see us checking in at 6:30 a.m., and even more surprised, I suspect, when we asked for separate rooms.

That morning, with only a couple of hours of sleep, I called Franklin Adams, chairman of the trustees, told him what had happened, and asked him to call an emergency conference of the trustees two hours from then, when I would be on the Rossiter twins' plane back to Catherville. Adams and the trustee board secretary spent the next two hours tracking down all the trustees, and by good fortune, all but one were able to be on the call.

I began by saying I would ask for an emergency meeting only in extraordinary circumstances, but I believed that was just what we faced. The university had an incredible opportunity but only if action was taken immediately. I outlined our plan, adding that I wanted to announce the trustees' authorization of the fundraising campaign, but to make that authorization conditional on the Faculty Senate's acceptance of the Rossiter brothers' donations. I explained that I thought this would put such pressure on the Faculty Senate that it could not, in the end, fail to support the donations, though I recognized that there could be resistance, especially from students.

The trustees heard my proposal, and without hesitation, Adams moved that the board support the plan. A few trustees raised questions of detail—was it certain, for example, that the Rossiter brothers would provide the funding they promised even if the campaign did not reach its goal? "Yes," I responded, "they have given me a written commitment." It was quickly apparent that all trustees would endorse the plan, which they did with enthusiasm.

Then I asked the trustees to approve my enhancing Season's salary by $15,000 a year on the grounds that she would be responsible for publicizing the fundraising campaign as well as the university more generally. I did this in part because she really deserved the extra pay in light of her brilliant design of the plan and in part because the trustees are allowed to meet in executive session only if a personnel matter is involved. I wanted an excuse to keep this meeting confidential in case news leaked out that the trustees had a hasty conference-call meeting. The Nebraska law requiring three days' notice for personnel meetings would be violated, but the circumstances of this session made it unlikely that anyone would raise this issue.

By the end of the flight home, I managed to reach Anchor, the one trustee who had not been on the call, and when I told him what had happened, he said he supported the plan with pleasure. He even managed to say, for the first time, "Good job, Charlie."

Louis, Season, and I landed in Catherville in the late afternoon, in time for Season to release a press bulletin announcing to the community on each campus that there would be a campus-wide meeting in the auditoriums the following day and that the three Rossiter brothers would be involved and would answer questions after they spoke. It did not take long for protest groups to gather with the aim of preventing the brothers from speaking.

By the morning of the planned session, over three thousand students and faculty had gathered near the entrance to the Catherville campus auditorium waiting to get in. It was clear to the head of campus safety—who had quietly made certain that some of his officers in plain clothes had attended meetings of the protest groups—that the aim of those groups was to ensure that the brothers could not speak. One example was that "No blood money from the three little pigs" would be chanted when the Rossiter brothers walked on the stage.

Season and I then huddled with the heads of the campus police and public safety, along with the chair of the Faculty Senate, and presented our plan. As I expected, the chair of the Faculty Senate was hesitant at first, saying that the audience was clearly expecting to hear the brothers in person. As calmly as I could, I explained that no one would hear the brothers if they came in person because several thousand persons would be doing their best to disrupt them. In all events, at that time the twins were in California, and Louis was on his farm. Fortunately, the Faculty Senate chair was a relatively conservative engineering teacher, and after some discussion he agreed.

Season's inspiration became a reality without a hitch. Those in the packed auditorium were quiet when I walked onstage, expecting to hear chanting and see signs held up as soon as I introduced the Rossiter brothers. The other two campuses saw this via the internet in their auditoriums. I announced that the brothers could not be with us but would speak via Connect—the interactive internet platform that David and Samuel Rossiter had created—so anyone who wanted could ask questions. Season lowered a large screen, and Louis Rossiter started speaking before the audience could quite realize what was happening. The audience began murmuring, but not before Louis said forcefully that the first option for his brothers and him was to withdraw the scholarship endowment and just walk away from the university. That silenced virtually everyone. Then he spelled out the alternative, emphasizing that the Faculty Senate would have to support it before they would agree. As we had arranged, the chair of the Faculty Senate appeared on the divided screen to say that these two options would be posted on the university's website for the rest of that week, and the faculty would then be asked to vote.

Most of the audience was still stunned when I came on the divided screen again with the three brothers and asked for questions. Ushers with microphones were scattered about the auditoriums to enable those in the audience to ask their questions. For the first couple of minutes, no one said a word.

Then Sally Inowa, a Native American whom I knew was also one of the student leaders of the movement to obliterate the Rossiter name at Nebraska State, stood up. She took the microphone and asked, "Why weren't students consulted? The president keeps talking about student success as center stage at the university. That sounds very hollow right now."

We were naturally prepared for that question, and Louis handled it well. "You and everyone else—students, staff, alumni, and all those who care about Nebraska State—have the right to express your judgments," he said. "But the faculty are the lifeblood of the university. Your views, and those of other students, deserve to be heard and considered. But with all respect, students come, learn, and graduate. The faculty stay, many for their entire careers. They teach, do research, and help ensure the economic future of Nebraska. My brothers and I believe their judgments must be the deciding ones on this issue."

Another student then said he thought it was unfair to have the brothers broadcast their views rather than enabling the audience to see as well as hear them live. We had prepared for this one as well, and I said that if they appeared in person, the university would have to pay many thousands of dollars on security services at the auditorium, but I and the trustees would much rather spend that money on student scholarships. "Free speech is essential on this campus," I affirmed, "but there is no requirement in the First Amendment or elsewhere that mandates the speech be in person." That answer got some boos but nothing like a serious protest.

Then a faculty member at the School of Social Work, the only school that was not listed by Louis as targeted for support by the brothers, asked why that school was excluded. Again, I stepped in and said that right now the School of Social Work was in danger of losing its accreditation, and it was understandable that the Rossiter brothers were not interested in investing in a school that was in such precarious shape. "But," I said, "I am now able to announce that the trustees have given me conditional approval to launch Nebraska Forward, the largest fundraising campaign in the university's history. As I have discussed with the Faculty Senate, the campaign is tied directly to steps taken to further the university's academic agenda. I hope and expect that the School of Social Work will be in a position to benefit from the campaign. The trustees made clear to me, however, that the campaign launch is conditioned on approval by the faculty of the five hundred million dollars in donations by the Rossiter brothers. Without that approval, there will be no campaign."

There were a few more questions about the timetable for the campaign and how students and staff might be involved, but I was able to say, with little pushback from the audience, that those issues had yet to be resolved. Suddenly, there were no more hands raised, and I concluded the meeting with a thank-you to everyone who participated. We had dodged a bullet.

The next day, I met with the Faculty Senate executive committee and worked out a schedule for it to consider the Rossiter bothers' proposal. The faculty of each school would vote on the matter. The vote would be advisory only and not binding on any of the faculty senators.

Since so many faculty members had expressed outrage at the racist beginnings of the Rossiter fortune, I was not sure how this would come out. In fact, I feared there would be moves to remove the name Rossiter from Rossiter Hall and Rossiter Quadrangle as well as to reject the plan the brothers proposed and with it the brothers' scholarship endowment. For a few days, with the student newspaper trying to promote controversy by getting incendiary quotes from some faculty and students, the situation was tense. But then I heard the results of the school faculty meetings and learned that only the School of Social Work faculty had voted to oppose the plan, and even that vote was close.

When I met with the Faculty Senate executive committee a second time to finalize the schedule, virtually all its members made clear that the plan would be approved by the full Faculty Senate. That was exactly what happened. The only tense moment was when an amendment was offered to the motion to approve the plan. The amendment would have called for the Rossiter name to be removed from Rossiter Quadrangle because Clarence Rossiter was "not a hero but a villain in the founding of the university" and should not be honored.

After some heated debate, a replacement amendment was proposed to add a plaque on the front of the Administration Building, which is part of Rossiter Quadrangle. The plaque would explain the history of the university's founding, including the massacre of Indians, the forced removal of the Chano Tribe from the land where the university was built, and the role of Clarence Rossiter in these events. The replacement amendment was adopted by voice vote. The meeting ended quickly after that, and I even received compliments for helping to attract so much funding for the university. Over and over, as senators spoke, they made clear that they would support the plan only because it included such a significant donation for a Native American Studies Center, scholarships for Native American students, and funding for new Native American faculty. In something of an anticlimax, by a four-to-one margin, the entire faculty approved the plan announced by the Rossiter brothers.

11

I could finally come up for breath after what I privately called "the Rossiter Crisis" was resolved and the fundraising campaign was launched. Fortunately, the ad for a new athletic director / football coach was running during the preceding month, and the search could not have moved forward during that period. The ad made clear that prior experience as a winning football coach was essential and that experience as an outstanding athletic director was strongly preferred, but, in all events, the successful candidate needed the skills and talents to be an effective athletic director.

Just as Eliot predicted, we received many applicants, a total of sixty-two. But as he also predicted, when he and his colleagues went through the résumés of those candidates, most of them lacked the qualifications for the job. At some schools, the football and overall athletic programs were too small. Some had poor football records. And some had been at their campuses too briefly to be considered seriously. Three had no experience in either position but apparently believed they, nonetheless, deserved to be considered. One was a high-level NCAA official, one a senior vice president at Nike, and the third a former deputy head of the US Olympics Committee.

Based on the screening by the search firm, Eliot recommended eleven candidates for search-committee review. Six had been football coaches and were now athletic directors. The other five were football coaches who might have the qualities to become a strong athletic director. I wanted the committee to narrow the list of eleven to no more than four or five to be asked for letters of recommendation, which would be read by the search committee before an interview.

As promised, the search firm had posted on the confidential website résumés and cover letters from each of the sixty-two candidates. In the cover letters, candidates were asked to explain their experience and why they thought that experience would make a right fit for Nebraska State.

At the committee meeting, I reviewed what I had done with the search firm to reduce sixty-two candidates to eleven and said that we would consider each with the aim of reducing the number we would want to interview. I reminded everyone that I had made a public commitment that the committee would interview at least one Black and one Hispanic candidate and said I was pleased that among the eleven, we would consider two candidates who were Black and one who was Hispanic.

Finally, I emphasized that all we had at this point were the applicants' résumés along with their cover letters. We would review these files and narrow the list as much as we could. Then we would ask the remaining applicants for letters of recommendation from three or four individuals with whom they had worked. Eliot and his colleagues would talk to those whom the applicants listed as recommenders, along with other individuals who worked or had worked for each candidate and persons for whom the candidate worked or had worked. The last step would be on-campus interviews for the small group of finalists.

At my request, Eliot presented each candidate in alphabetical order to the committee. Loren Backer came first, currently football coach at Boise State University. He had been the assistant football coach at that university before becoming head coach. After five years, he was promoted to be athletic director as well as football coach. Boise State had put football at center stage, not just in intercollegiate athletics but, insofar as I could tell, in everything else. And this worried me.

Sure enough, no sooner had Eliot finished reviewing Backer's background than Zanza said with enthusiasm in his voice, "I think he sounds perfect. Boise State punches way above its weight in football, and in my book, that's the key." Trustee Tyler immediately agreed. Then Ruth Stein, coach of the women's soccer team, spoke up. "Well, I don't know anything about Boise State except that it's in Boise. But any university where football is as dominant as was just suggested, worries me. We should want a new athletic director who cares for all sports and, most important, for the students who play all sports." Angel Samson, the physical therapist, echoed those comments and added her con-cern about football injuries. I asked if others wanted to speak, and Ron Savage, the athletic director of Oklahoma State, said he also thought the Boise State athletic program was unfairly tilted toward football to such a degree that the other sports were often on life support. This was probably not of Backer's doing, said Savage, but he thought it would be risky to expect a football coach who had worked only in that environment to give all sports at Nebraska State the attention they deserved. My clear sense was that Backer's supporters included only Zanza, Tyler, and Brian Sampson, the captain of the football team. Not even Lederer, the assistant football coach, seemed enthusiastic.

I wavered before stating my own views. The last step I wanted to take was to hire another Knowland. But we had no knowledge whether Backer was really in the Knowland mold. Given Tyler's strong support, I thought the better part of wisdom was to give Backer an interview with the hope that he would self-destruct. "Let's tentatively decide to give him an interview and move on," I said.

Ben Bandhurst, the football coach at Eastern Michigan University, was next. Lederer spoke up and said he knew one of the assistant coaches at Eastern Michigan, who told him that Bandhurst was a difficult personality, with an explosive temper.

"How can you be sure that your informant is not just trying to keep Bandhurst from moving?" Savage asked.

"I can't," Lederer responded. "But he's a good friend, and I don't think he would lie."

No one spoke up in favor of Bandhurst, and I assumed, correctly as it turned out, that we would not invite him for an interview.

Then came Charles Daly, the Black athletic director and former football coach at Stetson University in Florida. Carlos Castro spoke first.

"I applaud your eagerness to interview minority candidates," he said, "especially one who has been both football coach and athletic director. I might not have been considered by Minnesota State but for the fact that I am Hispanic. But I think I have done a good job there, and apparently so does the leadership of the university, for my appointment was just renewed for another five years, even though the president and I are not on the best of terms. I do not know anything about Daly, other than his credentials, and he may well not be the person we are seeking. I checked the records of the football team and then the whole athletic program while Daly has been the leader, and that record is solid if not great. I, for one, hope we will interview him. It could not have been easy to overcome the hurdles he must have encountered in Florida being a Black coach and then athletic director."

What Carlos said obviously had an impact because I saw nodding heads around the table, and no one objected when I said let's interview him.

Next came Robert Ender, from Eastern Pennsylvania University, and Adam Hamper, from Western Michigan University. By happenstance, each had a feature I knew would draw the attention of both Zanza and Tyler. Ender was obviously gay. His résumé made clear his presidency of the Gay Rights Advocacy Group on his campus, and his cover letter referred to his husband. Hamper was physically disabled for life, which was apparent because a picture of him accompanying his résumé showed him in a wheelchair, and he had participated in the Special Olympics as a tennis player. In an effort to head off discussion of those features, I underscored to the committee that both the law and university policy precluded us from taking into account either sexual orientation or physical infirmities. Zanza quickly responded, "Yes, but if those features limit a person's abilities to do the job, then they need not be considered." Zanza was right, but I knew this meant controversy, and it did.

Ender had been football coach for the past eight years and had an excellent record. He was voted coach of the year twice in that period. That seemed like a strong record to me and, as it turned out, to the other committee members, except Zanza.

"How can a gay guy go into the locker room and watch guys get naked without getting a hard-on," he said. "Oops, sorry about the term. But you all know what I mean. A gay guy can't be able to keep his sexual orientation, or whatever you call it, to himself. And he can't gain the respect of a bunch of tough Nebraska State players, any more than he would have gained my respect."

Even Tyler blanched at this outburst. "I won't go along with that," Tyler said. "But I do have doubts about this guy's abilities. We have other good candidates. Let's just give this one a pass."

But one after another, every other committee member spoke up in favor of Ender. "We are going to interview him," I said when the discussion ended.

Hamper was a different story. He had been football coach at Western Michigan and had a decent, but not great, record there. He had never come close to winning his conference championship. But after he had coached football for nine years, six as assistant coach and three as head coach, he was in a terrible, head-on car accident with a drunk driver. He almost died, but after multiple operations, he was able to come back to work, and this time his university chose him to replace the just-retired athletic director. His legs and one arm were paralyzed, as we learned from Eliot. But Eliot suggested we consider him because "he must have incredible grit to not only survive the crash but come back to work in his new position."

Even I had trouble imagining Hamper as the man we wanted. If we had been searching for just an athletic director, he might have been fine—even great. But to be an effective football coach seemed impossible given the times that coaches need to move up and down and around the football field in practices and in games. So I said just that.

"In this case, I think his physical limitations probably preclude his being right for us." Nodding heads indicated that everyone else was in silent agreement. We avoided another Zanza controversy.

But I added that I wanted to check with our general counsel, Norman Oreland, to learn if we would be violating the Americans with Disabilities Act for rejecting Hamper based on his disability.

"No surprise," Zanza said. "What an absurd idea. Why ask? We might not get the answer we want."

"Yes, I responded. But that's a risk I believe we have to take. I think we have an obligation to check, though I recognize that a football coach who cannot walk seems a bit unreal. Yet he applied, and I believe we at least owe him my checking with our counsel."

Next came Roger Jones, who was athletic director at Southern University and A & M College, a historically Black university. Jones himself was Black. At first there was silence because only a few on the search committee had even heard of that university. But as Eliot talked about his university, it became clear that not only was that campus a Division I institution, but it was also a member of the Southwestern Athletic Conference, and its twenty-two teams played competitively with other conference members. As a result, with no additional comments, the consensus was to keep him on the list.

We rejected George Cohen, football coach at Illinois State University. I assumed from his name that Cohen was Jewish, and as Nebraska State's first Jewish president, I amused myself by thinking that Cohen was our Jewish candidate. Affirmative action for Jews was not needed in the university world, though there had been an earlier time when there were quotas on Jewish students at major universities like Yale and Princeton, and Jewish presidents were virtually nonexistent. But we rejected Cohen because his record as coach was not a strong one.

Santiago Mateo, football coach at Southern Alabama University, was Hispanic and seemed like a stellar candidate. His teams had done well during his twelve-year tenure at Southern Alabama: they twice won conference championships and went to four bowl games. There was no question after Eliot presented Mateo's credentials that he would be interviewed.

Richard Mondran, football coach at Radford University, followed. I knew Angela Sampson, concerned about football and the injuries that resulted, would weigh in on this candidate, and she did. She had found an article in the student newspaper claiming that football players on the Radford team had more injuries than any other team in its conference. Zanza tried hard to defend Mondran, but he had already antagonized many on the committee, and when I asked for a straw vote, Zanza was alone in supporting him.

Eliot then told us that the last two candidates he had planned to propose had withdrawn. Presumably, they had told their universities that they were considering leaving, and those campuses countered with attractive offers that made both agree to stay.

After two exhausting days, I was able to say we had met our first challenge and had five candidates to move forward to the next phase: Loren Backer, football coach at Boise State University; Charles Daly, athletic director and former football coach at Stetson University; Robert Ender, football coach at Eastern Pennsylvania University; Roger Jones, athletic director and former football coach at Southern University and A & M College; and Santiago Mateo, football coach at Southern Alabama.

Two of those candidates were Black, and one was Hispanic. Santiago Mateo had been added to our initial list by Peter Zanza, and I went out of my way to thank him for suggesting Mateo. Zanza had heard about Mateo from one of his former roommates, who now lives in Alabama. I remember what Zanza said to me: "As you know, football is king in Alabama, and Mateo has done extremely well at Southern Alabama University. And he's Hispanic!"

I reminded the committee members that everything that had been discussed was confidential and said we would meet again to interview the candidates as soon as Eliot and his colleagues could get letters of recommendations from the applicants and interview others who worked with or for the candidates or supervised them. We would try to do all the interviews in one day, but that might not be possible because it depended on the interviewees' schedules as well as our own. In the next few days, I told the committee, Frank Eliot and his search firm associates would call the candidates whom we had not chosen to interview, thank them for their applications, and tell them we decided they were not the right fit for Nebraska State.

I knew the interviews and recommendation checking would take at least two weeks. The bad news was that the search had already taken more than four months. As a result, we could not begin the interviews until the last month the trustees had given me to find a new football coach and athletic director. The good news was that I could focus for the two-week break on urgent issues facing the university that had nothing to do with athletics. These included a board of trustees meeting and a tough session with the Nebraska legislature, which had decided on a 16 percent across-the-board cut in funding for all public universities, including ours.

Less than a week after the committee met, Frank Eliot called with some more bad news. His associates had been checking the credentials of each of the five candidates whom we would interview. This was standard procedure for searches. All too often, the process resulted in learning that one or more applicants for a position had exaggerated or even falsified her or his credentials. Sadly, that is what Eliot learned about Santiago Mateo.

In his résumé, Mateo listed that he had graduated from West Point, where he had played football, and then served six years in the army, rising to the rank of captain. He left the army to become a football coach and then athletic director at Butte Community College in Oroville, California, before being hired in that same role by Southern Alabama University. His football teams had done spectacularly at Butte, where they had won six conference championships and gone to eight bowl games. The record of his football teams for the last four years at Southern Alabama University was not as strong, but they had won more games than they lost, and most of the rest of the teams—women's as well as men's—had done well.

In checking with West Point about Mateo, however, an associate of the search firm found out that he had been dishonorably discharged from the army after a court-martial for sexually assaulting an enlisted woman. Fortunately, West Point keeps records of its graduates. When

I heard this news, there was no question in my mind that we needed to drop Mateo from our list of interviewees. I called Peter Zanza to tell him this news. At first, he started to argue with me, saying, "The dishonorable discharge was over a decade ago, and we have no reason to believe that Mateo had anything other than a clean record since this."

"But," I responded, "there is no way Nebraska State can afford to hire a person to be in charge of many women as well as men in the athletic department knowing, as we now do, that he was guilty of sexual assault. I am surprised he was not sent to military prison for his offense."

Zanza argued with me for a bit but finally said he understood my decision even though he might not agree with it.

Frank Eliot said he would call Mateo and tell him we knew about his dishonorable discharge and offer him the chance to withdraw his application. I answered that this was fine, but I was weighing whether I had an obligation to tell the president of Southern Alabama University what we had learned about his football coach.

"I thought you would raise that issue," Eliot said, "and you should know that when I talked yesterday to Mateo, he said he would withdraw his application but pleaded with me not to tell anyone at his university the reason." Eliot responded that the decision, of course, was mine but quoted what Mateo said: "I made a mistake, a serious one. I was drunk, a female sergeant was drunk, and we fell into bed together. Since I left the army, I have completely rehabilitated myself, no longer drink, and have a wonderful wife and two children. My wife knows nothing about my dishonorable discharge. Please do not let my university know about my one mistake. I might lose my job here as well as having to withdraw from your search."

I weighed the dilemma for a couple of days and decided I had to call the president of Southern Alabama University and tell him what we had learned about Mateo. If our positions had been reversed, I knew I would want him to call me. The president sounded shocked when he heard my report. "Santiago has been a wonderful athletic director since he came here," he said, "and I have heard only rave reviews about him from coaches and alumni."

"Well," I told him, "it's certainly your decision as to what you do with the information I just told you. Maybe Mateo really is completely rehabilitated, and you feel justified in keeping quiet about what you learned."

Then he asked me what I would do if our situations were reversed. I had considered just that issue and had no doubt about how to respond. "I would fire him," I said, "since he both lied on his résumé and committed a most serious offense. If we were to hire him, and the reason for his army discharge came out later, I might well be the one to be fired. But even more important, I think it would be wrong to bring him to our campus knowing what we know." The president said he could not exactly thank me for giving him this problem but realized it was the right thing for me to do.

The next day, I wrote to the committee members telling them that Mateo had withdrawn his application "for personal reasons." I was troubled that we would no longer be able to interview a Hispanic applicant, as I had committed to do, but felt that we had made the effort, and that would have to do.

Finally, I had time to check with Norman Oreland, our general counsel about Hamper, the candidate who was disabled. I knew enough not to put anything in writing that might later turn up in a trial, so I called Oreland and set out the issue. He promised to research the matter and be back in touch soon. He was as good as his word and called me at eight o'clock the next morning, though it was Saturday, and asked if he could come to the president's houses. Of course, I agreed.

"I have learned a lot about the Americans with Disabilities Act over the years I have been in this job," he said when we met, "but this is a new one to me. At first, I thought, why not? We don't reject a brain surgeon for never having had a brain tumor. What is so different, especially since the head football coach has assistants who can run up and down the field? Football is imbedded in our brains as a healthy male-only sport, but that does not make it right. Then I said to myself, 'Get real. You are looking for a sharp shift in Nebraska State football from Knowland's reign of terror—but without forgoing its winning ways. This is just a bridge too far. I doubt anyone will even raise the issue.'"

Oreland then added, "And my view is the same, incidentally, for not considering women in the position even though there may be—someplace—a woman football coach." The possibility of a woman coach was the question I ducked at the press conference when I took over as chair of the search committee, although I knew we would not have a woman football coach. I was relieved to accept Oreland's counsel, and he was right that no one ever raised the issue.

That same day, just as I was ready to post a note on the search committee's confidential website about Oreland's advice, Frank Eliot called me to say Mateo had withdrawn from the search. This was the message Hamper sent to Eliot: "This is a wonderful opportunity. But, on reflection, I realize that you need someone who is prepared for the stress of Nebraska State football in the wake—that seems the right word—of Coach Knowland. And that stress is more than I want to take on right now."

A few days later, Castro called me. He reminded me that his wife, Sofia, was having a show of her paintings in one of the Catherville galleries. It was not the gallery where my wife worked, otherwise she might have known her, though Sofia's last name was Garcia, not Castro.

"If you are coming with her to help set up the show, please stay in the president's house," I told him. "We have plenty of room, and it will be a chance for our wives to get to know each other, though you and I will probably be too busy to have much spare time." Castro said he was delighted to accept.

As it happened, Emma was coming back that afternoon with our twins from a mini vacation to New York. They had decided to go at the last minute, Emma told me, and I had heard only sketchy details of the plans. The girls had never been to New York, and this would be a real treat for them. They wanted to hear *Tosca* at the Metropolitan Opera. And they would have time for a visit to the Museum of Modern Art.

Castro and his wife, Sofia, came at midday, left their suitcases in one of our guest rooms, and went to supervise the hanging of her paintings. They returned in time for dinner. Emma and I found we liked Castro personally as much as I liked his wisdom as a committee member. And we both found Sofia delightful. She was a small, compact woman with a radiant smile, long black hair, and lots of jangling silver jewelry. She was born in Chile, and her family came to Minnesota when she was a child. Much of the talk at the dinner table was about art. It turned out that Emma and Sofia were fans of the same artists, particularly the abstract artist Helen Frankenthaler.

Castro said nothing at dinner about his job, but Sofia made clear that he was unhappy because he too often crossed swords with his president when the president tried to micromanage the athletic program. "He comes home too often," she said, "feeling depressed, much as he loves sports." Castro did nothing to deny what she said.

12

My first step during the two-week break from the search was to take a long weekend with Emma and our two girls. We went camping in Nebraska National Forest, hiked each day, and reminded ourselves how much we cared for each other. I had grown up hiking in the mountains and forests of New Hampshire and Vermont and loved the sense that hiking gave me of being completely away from whatever were my current headaches. Our twins started camping with me at age five and loved it as well. Each summer they went to a summer camp in Fairlee, Vermont, called Aloha. Emma, having lived in New York City until we were married, took some time before she could really enjoy hiking but had become as avid a fan as I was. We carried all our food, a small stove, two lightweight tents, and sleeping bags. We had a wonderful time.

After that quick break, I presented the university budget to the legislature and proposed a new plan that would enable public universities to expand their faculties. Under the plan, if a university raised half the endowment for a new faculty position, the state would fund the other half—up to ten new faculty members for any one university.

We had a fundraising campaign underway, and I felt confident we could meet that fundraising challenge. The University of Nebraska at both Omaha and Lincoln endorsed the proposal, but the smaller public campuses, Chadron State, Peru State, and Wayne State, opposed it on the grounds that they did not have the alumni bases to raise the necessary funds. I quietly negotiated a deal that those three campuses could join to raise funds and then share the new faculty that were hired as a result. The deal would have allowed the three smaller campuses of the University of Nebraska and of Nebraska State to do the same. But the legislature refused to fund the plan on the grounds that it was too expensive.

In concert with the other public colleges and universities, I then switched gears and proposed that the state match funding for new campus buildings. This was much more attractive to the legislators, for buildings are capital expenses and do not show up on the regular budgets. This plan was adopted, though modified so that the smaller campuses had to raise only one-third of the costs of their new buildings.

Then I could turn my full attention to the two major matters that were center stage for me—overseeing the academic agenda and the fundraising campaign. The first was going well; the second was not. The faculty teams for each school were shaping their academic priorities, and the central university committee was reviewing their plans. I saw clear evidence that the planning process had already strengthened the academic enterprise on each campus.

But our campaign fundraising efforts had stalled. We had the Rossiter brothers' gifts, which totaled $500 million, but the campaign to raise the additional $1 billion had gotten off to a slow start. We had set up a campaign committee, and I had planned campaign visits in every major city in the country where we had wealthy alumni, and that meant about twenty-five cities. We had raised about $223 million, but I had hoped at that point to be much further along in the campaign. The search had put a temporary stop to the tour.

Just as I was about to start focusing on this priority, Polly Porter rushed into my office to tell me that one of our students, Bussaba Carlan, had committed suicide. I had been worried about this possibility for some time. We have an excellent health service, but about 20 percent of our students need mental health counseling at some point during their undergraduate careers, which was average among major universities.

I spent much of the next two days finding out all the facts of what had happened. My office worked with the county coroner's office, which confirmed that she had committed suicide. She had been given sleeping pills by our health service when she complained of insomnia, and the pills heightened her anxiety. This made it harder for her to sleep—a vicious cycle. Apparently, she had stored up three dozen pills and swallowed them all in one sitting. This was enough, sadly, to stop her heart.

Carlan was from Thailand and in her senior year. She was planning to go on to medical school. (I later learned that Bussaba means "flower" in Thai.) It was spring break, and she was living alone on campus, as were many of our other international students. My office tracked down one of her roommates, Abby Bennett. Bennett said she knew Carlan had been worried about her grades and feared she would not get into medical school. Carlan was most worried about disappointing her parents.

My office called the US embassy in Bangkok and asked for help in locating the student's parents. We had their address but no way to reach them quickly by phone. The embassy found the number, and I called to tell Carlan's father and mother the heartbreaking news. I simply said that I very much regretted to tell them that their daughter had died.

They immediately asked, "What happened? What happened? Why didn't you protect her?"

As calmly as I could, I explained that she had committed suicide. They pressed for the facts, and I had to say that she took an overdose of sleeping pills. As they kept demanding more facts, I admitted that the pills came from our health service. The father got angrier and angrier on the phone, while the mother was simply sobbing. Finally, the father said they would take a plane in the morning and come to the campus to take the body of their child home. I offered to send a car to meet them at the airport and further to have them stay at the president's home. But he would have none of it. "We'll just be there," he said and hung up. I immediately called Norman Oreland to tell him what had happened and that we might have a lawsuit on our hands as well as a tragedy. He said he would try to find out all the facts from our health service but warned me that confidentiality rules might make that difficult.

I also called Sally Bennett, Carlan's roommate, and asked her if she would lead a student fundraising campaign for a scholarship fund in the name of Carlan. She quickly agreed, and by good fortune she used Facebook to raise over $65,000 in just two days. I told Bennett that I would also allocate enough additional university funds for the full scholarship. And I asked her to be ready to talk with Carlan's parents.

Two days later Carlan's father and mother walked into my office in the early afternoon. They had flown from Bangkok to Chicago and then from Chicago to Omaha, where they hired a car and driver and were driven straight to the campus. As a result, they went for over forty-eight hours with little sleep. When I said they must be exhausted, they brushed my comment away. They had called ahead to say when they were arriving, so I was able to alert the head of our health services to ask the doctor who had prescribed the sleeping pills to come to my office.

As soon as the parents sat down and I said how much I regretted what had happened, the father started to yell at me that the university had an obligation to take care of their daughter, the light of their lives, and the university had failed to meet that obligation.

I said I wanted them to hear from the doctor, Samantha Magrit, who had treated their daughter, and also from their daughter's roommate. Dr. Magrit made clear that Carlan had started coming to the health center eight months earlier in a state of great anxiety that meant she could not sleep. Dr. Magrit then prescribed the sleeping pills. They talked once a month after that, when Carlan came to receive a new supply of pills. The father broke in to ask why he was not notified, and Dr. Magrit explained, "Federal law precludes the university health center from telling others, parents included, about the health issues of patients unless the patients give permission, and Carlan specifically said not to notify her parents. But I can tell you, Carlan said she felt better the last time we had talked."

I then arranged a Zoom call with Bennett, who told the parents what a lovely human being their daughter was and how close their friendship was. "I knew of her anxiety and that she was taking sleeping pills, but she was such a happy person, so warm and friendly, I would never have imagined that she would take her own life."

First the mother and then both parents burst into tears and kept crying for a long time, saying nothing while Bennett told about various good times that she and Carlan had enjoyed living together. "I especially recall a time when we worked together for an entire weekend preparing a puppet show for children in this county using Thai puppets that we borrowed from a well-known collector in Lincoln I had read about."

Even though it was spring break, Bennett and Carlan had talked just three days before Carlan's death. Bennett stressed she had had no inkling of the seriousness of Carlan's situation. Dr. Margrit said this was all too familiar among students who committed suicide—no real warning signs.

Before Bennett left the call, I asked her to tell the parents about the new scholarship fund. She said she had spent the past day calling students in her dorm, how saddened they all were, and that every student in the dorm was contributing to the scholarship fund. I added that the university would provide the rest of the funds needed to endow the scholarship.

The parents were clearly deeply moved by what the roommate had said. They were silent for some time before the father stood up and said to his wife that it was time to go, to arrange to bring their daughter's body home to Thailand for a funeral. As he left, he said that he and his wife would like to give the funds for a second scholarship in their daughter's name. I thanked them, and they left. Saddened as I was by what had happened, I felt we had handled this tragedy as well as we could.

A few other problems occurred before it was time for the search committee to meet for interviews with the five finalists. But only one was a crisis—at our School of Social Work. I knew in general terms when I was Business School dean that the School of Social Work was in trouble. It had three deans in four years, and I had heard rumors of faculty and student discontent. But I had no idea the school's problems were so serious until I became president. Enrollments were steadily dropping, and the provost, Jenways Rogers, had told me he had heard the current dean was viewed with deep disdain by the faculty.

Sure enough, the social-work faculty voted no confidence in the dean at the same time as a group of school students staged a sit-in in the dean's office demanding better clinical placements. It was a mess, and both the student newspaper and the local media kept up a drumbeat of negative reporting from unhappy faculty, students, and alumni.

Rogers came to me the next morning to tell me in detail what he thought. "The school had an emergency visit from its accreditation agency," he said, "and the problems the agency reported were worse than I realized. Relations between the senior and junior faculty are in chaos, with the former essentially refusing to talk with the latter, let alone mentor them as senior faculty are supposed to do.

"I met yesterday with the junior faculty, and some began by telling me that they were not comfortable sharing their honest views with me because they feared retaliation. The charged atmosphere had continued, with many troubling comments indicating a lack of even the minimum level of what I term faculty culture. My sense of an extraordinary lack of collegial support among the faculty was further confirmed when I talked with three faculty members in other schools who worked with faculty in the School of Social Work.

"When I met separately with the school's senior faculty, they admitted quite candidly that they had not given junior faculty the support they needed. They blamed the dean—and prior deans—for promoting a climate of divisiveness. Then I talked to the dean, who was unable to go to her office because students were sitting in there. The dean sounded totally exhausted and said she could not handle the stress of the job and was resigning effective immediately. The only good thing that happened is that when I sent word to the students who were sitting in the dean's office that the dean had resigned, the students left, on my commitment to work to help find better clinical placements."

Rogers went on to describe two problems in the school that made matters worse. "First, three-quarters of social work classes are taught by adjunct faculty. While the average teaching load of the junior faculty is four courses a year, which is reasonable, the average for the senior faculty is less than two courses a year. Second, there are an extraordinary number of separate programs within the small school. I called a couple of members of past search committees for a dean of the school and learned that the candidates for the position uniformly believe that the department has too many programs. The main purpose of at least some of the programs, they told me, seems to be to enable senior faculty to head a program and, on that basis, be allowed released time from teaching."

"What a mess," I said. "What do you recommend we do?"

Rogers outlined two options. "The first is that the university phase out the School of Social Work as soon as practical and consistent with relevant university policies and procedures and obligations to current students. The disturbing situation I've described shows no sign of changing, and I now understand it is the cause of multiple failures of past searches for a school dean. I do not believe that a new search will lead to any better result than those searches. Substantial energy and efforts of faculty members and administrators, both inside and outside the school, would be expended, as in those past searches, all to a similarly futile result. I have made mistakes regarding the school, mainly in not getting on top of its problems sooner, but the reality is that an enormous amount of time by me and my office has been devoted to the school, and those are scarce resources. Social workers are in great demand these days, and after a few years, perhaps the school could be restarted with new faculty and new leadership.

"But I realize that closing a school is a huge deal, even a small school like social work. And I do see an alternative. First, you and I charge the social-work faculty to develop a set of common expectations that will serve them in their future guidance of the school, particularly in the mentoring of junior faculty by senior faculty and in reducing the number of the school's programs. Second, we charge the school's faculty to come together around a consensus candidate to lead the school—one chosen from within the school faculty—for at least the next three years. The school's problems will be less likely to multiply if the senior faculty is forced to confront those problems. And we should make clear that if the faculty are unable to fulfill those recommendations, then we will phase out the school. Finally, we will have to put some additional resources into the clinical placement problem, and I will come up with a plan to do that."

These clearheaded recommendations by Rogers reminded me how fortunate I and the whole university were to have him as provost. We talked back and forth about what to do, finally concluding that the second option was the least bad. As I told Rogers, we needed to try it before resorting to the first option, which would have been capital punishment for the school. We then continued to work out the details over the next two hours.

The whole incident reminded me how much I enjoyed being president of Nebraska State University. I took pleasure in helping solve tough problems such as this one, in ways that could make the whole university stronger. I loved leading efforts to enable students, faculty, and staff feel that they were a community larger and stronger than the sum of its parts. I knew I wanted to keep my job.

Even more significant, I realized that I had changed as a person since I started as president, especially since the search began for a new athletic director / football coach. I learned, for example, how to control my temper. Most important, I learned that my family was the center of my life, and I could not let my ambition corrode that center. I came to understand that I had to maintain a sound balance to my life that included both my family and my career, whether or not as president. Much as I wanted to stay as president, I could find another career and maintain that balance. I could never find another family.

13

Frank Eliot and his associates needed two weeks to arrange the necessary interviews for the four finalists. I was becoming increasingly nervous because time was running out on my tenure as president unless the committee and then the trustees agreed that one of those finalists would be a strong football coach and athletic director.

The day before the interviews were to begin, Porter told me Castro was on the telephone and wanted to talk to me. I immediately worried that Castro would tell me that he found himself just too busy and would have to drop his membership in the committee. The thought that this might happen depressed me because Castro had been the wisest and most helpful of all the committee members. He asked the best questions and made the most insightful evaluations of each of the candidates we had interviewed.

Porter gave me Castro's number, and I called him back. "I need to ask you something," he began. "I have watched the way you have led the committee and have been impressed by your efficient control of our meetings. You have respect for each member of the committee, even when some of their remarks are clearly off base. And, to be frank, I have been underwhelmed by the applicants we have reviewed. I don't understand how or why that has happened, but none of those we are scheduled to interview seem to me particularly strong. I know it is late in the process, but would you consider me for the position? I frankly think I could do a better job as your athletic director than any of those we have seen, and I would like to work for you and be part of the Nebraska State team."

I was stunned and silent for more than a minute. Then I responded, "Carlos, I would like nothing better than the chance to consider you as our athletic director and football coach. You have all the talent and wisdom to be a terrific leader for both our football program and all of Nebraska State intercollegiate athletics. But I made a promise to your president when he agreed to let you join the committee that I would not try to steal you. I cannot go back on my word."

"You would not be stealing me," he said. "I have come to you to apply for the job. To be frank, I find working for my president to be extremely difficult. I was in my job when he was chosen as president; otherwise, I am sure I would not have been hired, though he had to agree to renew my contract because our whole athletic program, including football, has been so successful.

"I will not say he is a racist, but he periodically makes remarks about Hispanic immigrants that make my blood boil. He also has a terrible temper and flies off the handle frequently for no real reason. He is a weak leader and demands I follow his whims and play favorites in the allocation of athletic department resources. He is also very difficult to work for, and I am confident you would be a pleasure to work for. Further, I have missed being football coach since I became athletic director and am confident I can handle both jobs successfully.

"I was impressed when you hired the first Hispanic associate athletic director in your conference and more impressed when I learned how you stood up to Knowland when his behavior was unacceptable. Knowland was a foul-mouthed bully, and you handled the situation as well as anyone could have."

I told Castro I was complimented by what he said, would think about the matter, and would call him the next day. But I knew even as I hung up the phone that I could not consider Castro for the job. I would not technically be "stealing" him, since he came to me, not the other way around. But the result would be the same. I put myself in the position of Castro's president and knew I would be furious, just as I was sure he would be. So I called Castro the next day and told him, with great reluctance, that I could not consider him because of my commitment to his president. He said he understood, though he was clearly unhappy at the news. When I said I would also understand completely if he decided he had to resign from the committee, he responded, "Of course, I won't do that. I'll just continue to try to help in every way I can to get you the best athletic director and football coach. I just wish it could be me."

At the outset of the committee meeting the day after Castro's call, I stressed my long-felt view that interviews are less important compared to in-depth discussions with a person's colleagues. "Too often," I said, "we get caught up in our first impressions of a person when we meet them and give much more weight to those impressions than to the experiences of those who have worked with a candidate. I'm often guilty of just that offense. But I'll try to keep reminding myself, and hope you will as well, to remember that a forty-five-minute interview often does not reveal much about an individual compared to what those who work with that person say.

"All too frequently," I said, "a candidate will have a great 'act 1, scene 1' in an interview without showing the limitations and weaknesses that are hidden in a brief conversation. An applicant may be articulate and charming but fail to have the strength of character to make tough decisions, and our new athletic director / football coach will certainly be required to make many tough decisions."

I suggested a brief list of questions we would ask all the candidates before opening the discussion to issues relating to a particular candidate. Most of these questions were the obvious ones: Why do you want this job? What in your background makes you think you have the right experiences to do the job well, particularly because it is really two jobs—football coach and athletic director? Why do you think you can manage both, and how will you be certain you can ensure a successful football program without undercutting other sports? What are your goals in your current job, and, particularly, how do you weigh having winning teams in comparison to other goals? How do you evaluate coaches and staff in your present job? (I told the committee that Knowland never did an evaluation, unlike Juarez, who did them with care.) How would you characterize your own leadership style? Describe a situation in which you made a substantial mistake and what you did afterward. I suggested that committee members take turns asking questions, which I hoped would give them a stronger sense of participation than if I had asked all the questions.

The interview schedules were based on when the four finalists could come to the campus. They were housed in four different hotels to minimize the chance that they would meet. We scheduled two interviews in the morning and two in the afternoon, to be followed by committee discussion, when, I hoped, we could come to a consensus on the right candidate. But I told the committee to hold a second day in case we needed more time.

Robert Ender, football coach at Eastern Pennsylvania State University, was the first to be interviewed. From the moment he started talking, I could tell he put everyone's teeth on edge. He was a big man with a huge belly that hangs out over his belt and partway down his thighs. And he had a high-pitched voice, almost a squeal. What he said seemed, at least to me, quite reasonable, but his overweight physical presence and voice made it hard to concentrate on what he was saying. He gave sensible answers to all our initial questions.

But then, A. J. Lederer, who was a trainer, asked, "Sorry to be personal, but how can you expect players on your teams to stay in good physical shape when you look so out of shape?"

There was silence for a minute before Ender responded. "I do my best," he said, "but I usually work late, grab too many snacks, drink too much beer, and have too little time for exercise."

At least he was being honest, but it was clear in that moment that he would not be chosen, though our questioning with Ender went on for the next forty minutes. He had good references from those with whom he worked, but we could not ignore his bulging belly or squeaky voice.

Roger Jones, from Southern University and A & M College, was next to be interviewed. He had a good-looking chiseled face and a modest, soft-spoken demeanor, which made it hard for me to imagine him as a football coach, as he had been before being athletic director. In my experience, most coaches yell at their players, at least in the locker rooms. Those coaching basketball, women's as well as men's, are the loudest yellers, with football coaches not far behind.

Jones talked about his background in rural and segregated Arkansas, going to a small school there, playing fullback on the high school football team, and then getting a full scholarship to the University of Arkansas. He was one of only 18 students in his school out of a class of 170 who went on to college. The football locker room and field were the only places in the university where there was a critical number of Black students, apart from one all-Black fraternity. Jones made up his mind early as a freshman that he wanted to play professional football and said he had a good shot at doing so until he tore his Achilles tendon in his senior year and was never able fully to recover. He decided then to become a coach, which he did successfully for eight years, and that led to becoming the athletic director at his campus.

We knew the records of the football teams at the Southern University and A & M College over the four years he had been athletic director had steadily gotten worse, though they had been successful when he had been football coach. I asked him why before letting Zanza speak, for I knew Zanza would ask the same question in an accusatory way. Unfortunately, Jones had no good answer to that question, in fact no real answer at all. Zanza followed my question by asking why he had not fired his women's basketball and men's swimming coaches, both of whose teams won only one match in the last two years. Again, his answer was a lame one: "The students on their teams really like those coaches and tell me they learn a lot from being on the teams, and I think that is the most important thing." I could silently agree that was important, but abysmal records like those of the two coaches signaled real problems, ones Jones apparently ignored.

I was nervous about how the conversation would go among the committee when we talked just among ourselves. Would some members support him just because he was Black, or at least put a heavy thumb on the scales of judgment for that reason? I was relieved when Ron Savage, the athletic director from Oklahoma State, who had asked searching questions in every one of the interviews, said, "He seems like a really nice fellow, one with whom I would love to have a beer. But I cannot imagine him as either football coach or athletic director at Nebraska State. He's not tough enough." A few others spoke, echoing similar views, and Lederer, the assistant football coach, said he totally agreed. So Jones was out.

Next was Charles Daly, athletic director and former football coach at Stetson University in South Florida. A handsome Black man with a powerful build, he was our youngest candidate, at about thirty-five years old. He immediately came across as a bright and personable guy who had been a successful football coach and had made intercollegiate athletics at Stetson stronger. In answering our initial questions, he put an emphasis on his aim of building a deeper sense of community that linked the student athletes, the coaches and staff of the athletic department, and the rest of the college. He put a premium on finding ways to highlight each of the teams, women's and men's, and on encouraging Stetson's students, faculty, and staff to be boosters for those teams.

His technique was disarmingly simple, not unlike the suggestion made by Oneida Appletree, the Native American student government president on the committee. Daly polled the faculty about what were their favorite sports and found that all but a handful of sports played by teams at Stetson had at least one faculty member who was a fan. Daly took out a different ad in the student newspaper every few days at the beginning of the fall semester with a picture of a faculty member who supported a team, joined by the team coach and the team captain or captains. He limited each sport to one faculty member so that each sport would seem to have the same amount of faculty support. Each ad quoted the faculty member lauding his or her sport, encouraging students to come to the next team contest, and offering prizes for those who did. Daly found faculty members to support the few teams that were not already chosen. As a result, faculty members became excited about "their" teams.

All this and more sounded terrific, just the kind of entrepreneurial energy and initiative that we needed at Nebraska State. So what was the problem? It was, unfortunately, that it became all too clear from listening to Daly that Stetson University and Nebraska State University were so different that it could be tough to make the leap. Stetson had four thousand students while Nebraska State had forty thousand. He was a star in the small pond of a small campus and was doing well there. But I felt uncertain whether he could be a right fit at our university. Further, it was clear from Zanza's questions that he thought Daly would spend too much time being athletic director and not enough time being football coach. On reflection, however, I concluded that Daly could grow into the job at Nebraska State, because he had the necessary values and personal qualities. With the exceptions of Zanza and Tyler, the committee agreed with my view that Daly could handle being both athletic director and football coach.

Loren Backer, football coach at Boise State, was last to be interviewed, and before he even came into the room, Zanza said, "I know this guy is going to hit a home run." But instead, he struck out, as I had secretly hoped.

Backer was short and seemed almost as wide as he was tall, with powerful arms and a thick neck. He described his experiences on the football field at Boise State in glowing terms, but in a way that sounded just too good to be true, though we knew Boise had a very successful football program. Everything was "the best" and "so much fun," and "we're always a total community that always cares for each other."

After just five minutes, I became restless and, after ten minutes, irritated. When it seemed Backer could not stop talking, even to take a breath, Castor broke into his monologue to ask, "Please tell us about a time when you failed to do what you wanted to do as athletic director." Backer stopped and reflected for what seemed at least another five minutes but probably was just a minute. "I was trying to get the football team trainer to ensure that more fruits and vegetables were on the team's training table," he said. "But the trainer kept saying that this was a dietician's responsibility, one who had taken courses in good diets.

So I let the matter go even though I thought the trainer was wrong." I could just see eyes rolling on the faces of other committee members, all of whom, students included, had failed in something significant, just as I had, and felt the idea that this was Backer's most important failure seemed ludicrous. We let the interview go on for the full forty-five minutes, but I knew we were not going to choose Backer.

I was in a quandary about what to do. Our only real choice was Daly. I thought he could do an adequate job both as football coach and athletic director. But it was clear that neither Zanza nor Tyler believed Daly was right for the job, and I had qualms myself. Daly did not have the bullying, misogynistic dark side of Knowland, but he also lacked Knowland's charisma. I felt certain Zanza and Tyler would object to choosing Daly. If the committee majority approved him, as I thought likely, and I supported him, Tyler would persuade the trustees to reject him.

I decided to temporize and adjourned the session. "Let's all think about this issue overnight before we make such an important decision," I said. "We can come back at nine o'clock tomorrow morning and resolve it."

Just as I was leaving the meeting, Castro asked if he could call me at home that night. I agreed and gave him my private number. I then left the meeting with a heavy heart and told Emma my days as president were numbered. I was not enthusiastic about the only candidate I thought was viable and was sure that Tyler would effectively veto him if the committee approved him. Emma and I hugged each other, and then she had a big glass of bourbon, while I had one of scotch. We were silent for a while and then started talking about what might be next. Should I try to go back to the Business School as a faculty member? "In my gut," I told Emma, "I don't think I could do that. It would be too hard for me. I've been there, done that."

"Maybe," Emma said, "we should use the time that is left on your contract as president to explore the world and, in the process, think through our options together. I'll always have my art. And I'm confident you will find a new career—maybe in the nonprofit world. We'll be together; that's the important thing." I gave Emma a big kiss and held her tightly for a long time.

Castro called about an hour after I came home. He said he had resigned as Minnesota State athletic director. "I just couldn't take the lack of leadership from the president," he told me, "especially the racist innuendoes that he kept making. Now I hope it is not too late for you to consider me as Nebraska State athletic director since I am no longer at Minnesota State, and the president there cannot criticize you if you decide to hire me."

My immediate reaction was joy and relief. I had come to admire Castro greatly during the committee sessions. He seemed to have a solid command of what an athletic director should do and how to do it. And I knew his football teams had very strong records when he was coach, going to bowls almost every year. But, of course, I did not have evidence about how he worked with his coaches, staff, students, and alumni or his leadership style. "Let me think about this for a few minutes," I said, "and call you back."

After I hung up and thought briefly about the matter, the only question in my mind was whether I would be violating my promise to the president of Minnesota State not to steal Castro. But I concluded there was no rational basis for that president to feel aggrieved, since Castro was no longer his employee. So I called Castro back and told him I would be delighted to consider him.

I said I would explain to the committee that he had resigned from Minnesota State and wanted to be considered by our university. I would say I strongly favored doing this and ask if anyone objected. Assuming there was no problem, Eliot and his associates would do the same review of Castro's time as football coach and then athletic director at Minnesota State as they had done for the four finalists. We would meet in a week for an extra session. Naturally, Castro would resign from the committee. Castro said all this made sound sense to him. I closed by telling Castro that I was thrilled he wanted to come to Nebraska State, and while I naturally could not commit to hiring him, I had a good feeling about this prospect.

I then called the president of Minnesota State to tell him that Castro was a candidate for Nebraska State athletic director. At first, he was furious and suggested that I had a plan to steal Castro indirectly despite my promise not to do so directly. But I repeated the facts, and he finally calmed down. I think he also concluded he would look bad in the eyes of his fellow presidents and others if he went public with his complaints about me. He and I had never been friends before, and I was certain after this that there was no chance of friendship in the future.

At the start of the meeting with the committee, with Castro not present, I told the members exactly what had happened and asked if anyone had a problem with considering Castro and delaying our final meeting for a week while the search firm investigated him in the same way it had done the four finalists. No one objected, and I saw big smiles on a number of faces.

A week later, the committee met and learned that Eliot and his associates had interviewed over a dozen of Castro's colleagues. With only one exception, all of those interviewed were extremely positive. The one negative voice was the president of Minnesota State. He described a litany of concerns about Castro and said he would soon have fired him if he had not resigned. "First, and most important," Eliot read from notes of his interview with the president, "Castro never really accepted my authority. He always acted as though he knew so much more about athletics than I do that he did not need to listen to my views." The interview went on for a full half hour, but that point was repeated with different words and in various ways over and over. He never explained why Castro's contract was just renewed for the next five years given what he had said.

All of Castro's colleagues who were interviewed insisted that their names not be used because they feared retaliation by the president. But all were extremely enthusiastic about Castro and expressed their deep regret that he had resigned. Some of those interviewed were assistant coaches and staff when he was football coach. Others were current coaches and other staff members in the Athletic Department.

One after another, Eliot quoted statements that made clear Castro provided strong and effective leadership, instilled in both coaches and staff a sense that both the football program and the department as a whole could improve, and their individual and collective efforts were key to making improvement happen. Those statements also made clear that the department had steadily become stronger under Castro's leadership. Some gave hints that if Castro were at another university and wanted to hire them, they would be eager to work for him.

The interview itself with Castro was a joy. It was made easier, of course, because everyone on the committee knew and respected Castro, though they did not know the details of his background and experiences.

Like Juarez, our former associate athletic director, Castro was born in Mexico, and his parents immigrated to the United States when he was a young boy. But their paths diverged after that. His father joined the army during the Vietnam War and, as a result, was able to become a US citizen on a fast track, as were his mother and Castro. After twenty years in the army, his father retired, and the family moved to Boston, where his father worked for a security service.

Castro got a scholarship to attend Boston Latin School and played football there. He went to the University of Michigan on a football scholarship because of his abilities. After graduating, he played American-style football in Canada, and when that did not seem to be leading anywhere in terms of a career, he returned to the University of Michigan as an assistant football coach. At the same time, he earned a master's degree in sports management. Two years later he was hired as football coach at a small liberal-arts college in Michigan, and then, following four years in that job, he was selected as football coach at Minnesota State. After a successful coaching career at Minnesota State he was chosen as athletic director and had been in that position for six years when he resigned.

After summarizing his life story, Castro was asked why he had resigned. He explained that he had been hired by the former president of Minnesota State and had a strong relationship with her. (In an interview with her, Eliot heard her give Castro an enthusiastic recommendation.) But the current president, Castro said, was always trying to second-guess his decisions. And he barely hid what Castro thought were racist views, though Castro added that the president might not even be aware of how his statements could be interpreted as racist.

For the rest of the interview, Castro described at length his experiences as football coach, inheriting a losing program over the previous four years and turning it, in just one year, into a winning program for the remaining years he coached. He loved coaching football and only left to become athletic director because it offered new challenges, and the former president, whom he admired greatly, pressed him to do so.

After six years as athletic director, he felt confident he could do both jobs successfully at Nebraska State. He described his management style, how he chose coaches and staff, and how he had worked to strengthen the Athletic Department while expanding opportunities for students to play club sports if they were not talented enough to be on a varsity team. He made a point of stressing that he would not accept any player unless he thought there was a realistic chance that the player would actually play. "Far better to play on a club team than sit on the bench as a member of the varsity—better for the player's overall well-being and better for the team." Knowland had been committed to the opposite approach.

Castro had the advantage of having listened to the various concerns of search committee members, and he addressed his responses to those issues before being asked about them. For example, he expressed concern about injuries in all sports, particularly in football and rugby but also in other sports as well, and told about ways that his coaches and trainers had developed means to lessen injuries when players were practicing.

Zanza pressed Castro on whether he agreed that football was the most important sport. Castro responded that in terms of revenues, football clearly was most important, and it was certainly the sport that he cared most about. But he stressed that every sport was most important to the students who participated in that sport, and university athletics at every level should be about enabling students to enjoy playing while, at the same time, learning some of life's important lessons. When pressed about those lessons, he said that players, when well coached, learned to watch out for each other and to help each other, even in sports like golf and cross-country in which each person competed individually.

There was more, but by the end of the interview, the beaming faces of all the committee members made clear they thought Castro was the right person to be the next athletic director and football coach of Nebraska State. Zanza and Tyler had wide smiles, as did every other committee member. Castro left the room, and when I took a vote, it was unanimous.

I reminded the committee that they had agreed to total confidentiality and that I still had to negotiate a contract with Castro, which might take some days. As soon as the meeting was over, I asked Tyler to inform the other trustees and said that if they wanted an online meeting to hear directly from me about Castro, I would arrange that. But Tyler said he doubted that would be necessary.

The next day I called Castro. "I want you as our next athletic director," I said, "and the search committee unanimously supports that decision."

"I'm thrilled," Castro responded.

I told him I wanted him to take complete charge of both the football program and the athletic department and to consult me only when he had a problem he thought I could help him handle. Otherwise, I emphasized, I just wanted to return to my role as fan.

I offered Castro a compensation package that included $150,000 more in salary per year than he was making at Minnesota State and a five-year contract instead of the more usual three-year one. I knew I could have hired Castro for three years at the same salary as he had received, but I wanted him to come with the extra motivation that my offer would ensure. And the donation that David Rossiter had promised would ensure we had a new endowment for the football program that would more than cover this cost.

Castro said he would be willing to start in a week, although his family would not be able to move until his two sons, both in high school, finished school in the spring. His wife would stay with the boys until then. As I had planned, he said he would work with MacGruder for a couple of weeks before MacGruder moved to his new job.

Two people were as happy as I was when I called them and told them the news—Emma, who was always dubious about my taking on the role of chairing the search, and MacGruder, who was eager to start his new life at The Ohio State University.

Three days after Castro and I had signed his contract, we had a press conference, and I introduced Castro to the university. And I went back to work, promising myself that from then on, I would limit my involvement in Nebraska State intercollegiate athletics to being a cheerleader for all our teams.

At least for now, I thought to myself, academics are still the heart and soul of Nebraska State, and Nebraska State football had been returned to its role in providing fun for its fans. The label "student athlete" still has those two words in the right order.

As a last act, I reminded the search committee members that they had responsibility for choosing a new nickname for the Nebraska State football team, one that would replace "The Hogs." The student newspaper had published all the names that had been proposed, and a run-off election for students, faculty, staff, and alumni narrowed the list to ten names. The committee members discussed each one at the end of a raucous celebration dinner Emma and I held for them at the President's house. The voting was tense as ten names were reduced to six, and then three. The final vote was unanimous in favor on "Flying Colors." And a huge, multi-colored flag was designed to be raised at every football game.

The search had come off with flying colors.

Epilogue

Emma and I celebrated by going to the same hamburger joint we went to for our first date. We talked about what had happened and what we had learned. We kept reminding each other of the challenges leading up to the search and then during the search itself and how those challenges taught us to work together in ways we never had to before, and to handle the setbacks and frustrations of the last six months.

"It took us a while," said Emma, "to realize that your job was really our job. We had to learn to support each other when it seemed everything was headed south. We thought for a while that even Franklin Adams had deserted you. He didn't. Instead he gave you a chance to succeed against great odds."

"It was we who succeeded," I said. "You told me to stop feeling sorry for myself and, instead, make the search succeed in just six months, which seemed an impossible task. And you stressed we had a future together whatever happened in the search."

"You know how you told me about breaking the arm of your fraternity brother?" asked Emma. "And then I realized I had also lied to you—withheld the truth, which is the same thing—about the twins' friend who needed an abortion. We grew stronger that day and thereafter, and closer together, which is much more important."

Suddenly, as if on some cue from upstairs, a voice exploded from the TV on the wall above the hamburger cooker. "He fades back, he ducks to avoid a tackler, and then he throws. It's a long pass. Ceransky leaps up over the head of his defender and hauls it in—touchdown!"

I didn't know who was playing. And I didn't care. But I did know I had to talk about Knowland.

"I never would have thought that Knowland could have taught me anything useful," I said to Emma. "But I was wrong. During the search, I came to realize that he cared, really cared, about his players. Do you remember the stories that Tyson and the football captain told the committee? Knowland let Tyson stay in his home when Tyson had been unable to pay his rent. The captain said Knowland enabled him to play football better than he thought possible. And he said Knowland gave him pride in himself. And that that was something he'd never had before.

"I need to learn to care, really care, about my colleagues that way," I said to Emma. "Our family is the center of my being. But it can't be everything when so many around us need our help to reach their potential and take pride in themselves."

Knowland was a teacher, I thought, and not many teachers come away from their games with the kind of compliments given to Knowland. Yes, he was a terrible role model, a misogynist, and a bully. But he not only gave life lessons to his players; he gave Nebraska, particularly Nebraska State, a lot to cheer about. I would never have understood all that without the search. Knowland was not a good man. But he did good things—many of them. And making me a bit wiser was one of them.

For Indiana University Press

Tony Brewer, Artist and Book Designer
Gary Dunham, Acquisitions Editor and Director
Anna Garnai, Editorial Assistant
Brenna Hosman, Production Coordinator
Katie Huggins, Production Manager
Darja Malcolm-Clarke, Project Manager/Editor
Dan Pyle, Online Publishing Manager
Michael Regoli, Director of Publishing Operations
Pamela Rude, Senior Artist and Book Designer
Stephen Williams, Assistant Director of Marketing